SOUR NOTES

A NOVEL

D. K. WALL

Conjuring
Reality

All inquiries should be addressed to:

Conjuring Reality Media
65 Merrimon Avenue #1053
Asheville NC 28801
ConjuringReality.com

ISBN 978-1-950293-07-0 (Paperback)
ISBN 978-1-950293-08-7 (eBook)

Library of Congress Control Number: 2023910465

Cover designed by Glendon S. Haddix of Streetlight Graphics

ALSO BY D. K. WALL

The Lottery

Jaxon With An X

Liars' Table

Sour Notes

1

I wrapped my hand around the brass handle of my brother's casket and tightened my grip. Sweat trickled down the back of my neck, soaking the collar of my new dress shirt.

It wasn't really new, of course. The shirt was a hand-me-down from Dean. Mom insisted I wear it for the funeral. I didn't want to, but it wasn't the day to argue.

Being subjected to secondhand clothes as a little kid was bad enough, but how many eighteen-year-olds wore cast-off clothing from their brother? Their dead brother? Their twin brother?

We weren't identical, of course.

Dean was broad shouldered, muscular, and athletic. Just like the other five pallbearers surrounding the coffin, his high school football teammates. Or baseball. Probably both. I didn't know. I paid little attention to the dumb jocks that were my brother's friends. They noticed me even less.

The worst part about the shirt? It hadn't even been new to Dean. Mom had bought it for him to wear to church from the Goodwill store—when he was thirteen. Five years later, it was still too big for me.

Everyone at school had called him Big Mac. When he was ten and playing baseball in the park, Dean had hammered a home run. As the biggest kid on the team, he'd done that dozens of times.

But that particular hit was legendary—a resounding crack as the bat connected with the ball. It'd sailed over the fence, high enough to be picked up on the radar down at the Asheville airport. Or so the story went. In small towns, there wasn't much to do but tell tales. The facts didn't matter much. The one true part, for sure, was that it'd come down in the parking lot and smashed the windshield of a passing police car.

The tires squealed as the car screeched to a halt. The cop threw open the door and hopped out like he was being attacked, his hand on his holster. Instead of some terrorist threat, all he saw was a bunch of kids hooting and hollering.

He must have thought they were laughing at him, and that made him mad. He marched toward them, spitting and sputtering, and demanded to know who'd thrown the baseball at his car. That sent them into another fit of hysterical laughing.

The harder they tried to explain that it was an accident, the funnier it became to them. All they could do was point at Dean, who towered over the rest of them, with the bat draped over his shoulder.

The cop shook his head as he looked at the home plate then at his car. He pointed a finger at Dean and said, "You might be big, mac, but there ain't no way you hit it that far."

A nickname was born. The cop didn't know Dean's last name was McDougal, which made it funnier. Every kid was calling him Big Mac before they left the ball field. The tale grew as the kids shared it with their friends. People who hadn't even been at the park pretended they had, just to tell the tale. The association with a fast-food burger made it epic.

When the title floated through the halls of school, I naturally became Little Mac. I pleaded with them not to call me that, but the harder I begged, the more they did it. Dean didn't stop them. He reveled in his new brand too much.

Being Freddie McDougal was bad enough, but Little Mac was worse. Forever, I would be the little brother to the legendary Dean McDougal. I was little by forty-two whole minutes and a bunch of muscle.

"Ready, Little Mac?" Russ Caldwell turned his head so he could look over his shoulder and check on me. A decent guy, he was the nicest of the pallbearers. He'd grown up on the farm next door, so we had known him our whole lives. He was Dean's best friend and tolerated me because of it.

"Don't worry, Russ. I got it if he don't." Blake Torrence's loud whisper came from behind me.

My jaw clenched. Blake was a bully who loved picking on other kids at school and making their lives miserable. He left me alone—mostly—but only because I was Dean's little brother. Now that Dean was gone, who knew how long that would last?

When the preacher gathered us before the funeral, he'd sized me up against those five guys towering over me. The sleeves of the shirt billowed over my skinny arms. He'd suggested I serve as an honorary pallbearer and walk with my parents instead, and they would find another of Dean's friends to take my place.

He'd tried to make it sound special, but I knew what he meant. I couldn't handle it.

I'd argued. That was my brother in that box, damn it. Honorary wasn't good enough. I was determined to do my share. I needed to. All I had to do was carry the coffin through the church, down the front steps, and across the grounds to the far side of the cemetery.

How hard could it be?

Russ had stepped into the debate and suggested I walk

between him and Blake on one side, holding the center of the casket, so they could handle the weight for me.

That steamed me. He thought I couldn't do it, but the preacher had reluctantly agreed, and there wasn't any point in arguing any more. I would show them.

As I stood in front of all those people at the end of the service, my hand on that cold rail, doubt blossomed. The distance was long. The ground was uneven.

And the weight? Big ol' Dean McDougal and that monstrous box weighed more than I'd guessed. I had to carry it, though. I couldn't fail.

I took a deep breath and nodded. Russ shot a doubtful look over my head at Blake then faced forward.

We lifted. They grunted. I groaned. Even with their help, the weight was staggering.

The preacher led the horrible parade through the open double doors of the church. The wooden boards of the broad porch creaked under our feet as we exited the vestibule. A gentle summer breeze swirled and cooled my face, a welcome respite after sitting inside that stuffy building on those hard pews for the last two hours.

Teary-eyed classmates had extolled Dean's friendship. Coaches had celebrated his sporting prowess. Teachers had praised his presence in their classrooms. The principal had hailed his leadership as the senior class president. The preacher had capped it all off, exalting his sainthood of regular church attendance.

I'd declined to make my own speech. Not from a fear of public speaking. I wasn't a big fan of talking, but I could play my guitar and sing in front of strangers all night. Nothing rewarded me more than hearing an audience clap and sing with my songs or seeing them sway to the music and throw money in my open guitar case on a street corner in Asheville. I was good at busking. It had bought my piece-of-crap car.

But this was different. The church was filled with Dean's friends, not strangers. And they didn't want to hear the things I would have said.

The teachers never mentioned his dismal grades or the classes he'd skipped so he could go skinny-dipping in the river on warm spring days. The girls wailing about his demise didn't admit how many of them he'd bedded then ignored when he moved on to his next conquest. His buddies didn't discuss the pranks he had instigated or all the fistfights he'd been in. All the hell he'd raised around town never came up.

In all the talk about "the good die young" and "gone too soon" and "his whole life ahead of him," not a soul breathed a word how hours after our high school graduation party, Dean had driven his precious Chevy Silverado off a road and into a tree.

At least they didn't say it in the church. Not in front of my parents.

But I knew how small-town gossip worked. The same people singing his praises during the service had, no doubt, gathered in the days between the accident and the funeral in their little groups and expressed their misgivings and asked their questions. Questions that would get asked again tomorrow. People would talk about it until the next scandal distracted them.

"Hadn't Dean driven that stretch of road hundreds of times?"

"How did he lose control when it was perfectly straight?"

"How fast was he driving?

"How drunk was he?"

And I knew what they whispered when they looked at me. "Did you hear he got into a fight with Freddie earlier that night?"

Sweat dribbled into my eyes and blurred my vision, so I didn't see Russ descend the first step. The coffin tilted forward, shifting the weight of its awful cargo. My burning muscles buckled. I stumbled.

Russ and Blake moaned under the strain but held on to prevent a disaster. Blake's warning hiss came from behind me. "Keep it steady, Little Mac."

I never wanted to hear that nickname again. Every utterance reminded me of the gap between me and my brother. Not just size. Or that he could hit a baseball and I couldn't. We didn't have anything in common.

We didn't even share a birthday. Or birth month. He'd arrived just before midnight on April thirtieth. I'd come just after the flip of the calendar.

We lived way out in the country, my parents would patiently explain as we were growing up, so people didn't want to travel to our house twice for birthday parties. Besides, we couldn't afford to skip two whole days working the farm. They thought it easier to just pick a day and share the event. Since Dean's birthday came first, Little Freddie wouldn't mind celebrating a day early. After all, they'd ask, what difference did it make what day we picked to celebrate?

What they didn't say, but I knew, was that people would come for Dean's birthday but not mine. He rode ATVs, hunted, fished, played in the creek, did all the fun things that kids liked to do. Especially kids in Millerton.

Not me. My allergies would flare up. Or I would be recovering from some bug. Or maybe it was because I just preferred to stay inside with my books and guitars. No one wanted to hang out with boring Freddie.

I regained my footing, locked my eyes on the center of Russ's back, and followed him down the steps. Once we reached flat ground, I focused on the far side of the cemetery and the waiting catafalque beside the freshly dug hole.

We marched. Step after struggling step. One foot in front of the other. My muscles screamed for relief. As we neared our goal, the stench of dirt invaded my nostrils, reminding me of the recently tilled fields surrounding our house each spring. Dean loved driving the tractor and being out in the fields, working shoulder to shoulder with Dad. After a long day of sweat and toil, they would sit at the supper table, smelling like soil and chattering endlessly about insects, disease, yield, rain, and sun. I tried not to sneeze from the earthly assault.

My stomach flopped at a horrid thought—Dean would appreciate being one with the dirt for eternity. He had worked and played in it every day of his life.

We reached the bier and settled the coffin with a muffled thud. With a tilt of his head, the preacher motioned for us to line up beside him, just beyond the grave. We stood shoulder to shoulder in a rigid row—me a foot shorter than the rest—and watched the migrating congregation pick their way through the headstones.

Our parents led the mob. Skeeter and Libby were the current generation of a long line of McDougals who had farmed this valley. Fixtures at church and the farmers' co-op. Members of the PTA and booster club at the high school. Dad volunteered at the fire department. Mom organized the church bazaar. Pillars of the community. They always carried themselves with a quiet confidence, comfortable in the respect they commanded from the community.

Now, frail and broken, my parents leaned on each other, stumbling across the uneven ground. Ever since a sheriff's deputy knocked on our door Sunday morning with his grim news, they'd moved like lost souls through the rituals of a family death.

Mom had greeted each visitor—and there were many. She thanked them for the casserole or pie they'd brought, carefully labeling each bowl with a sticker so she could return it.

Dad had sat out in the barn, tinkering with the tractor and

pretending to work while his buddies hung out with him. They talked little, communing in their silence.

When he and Mom reached their waiting seats under the tent, Dad hesitated and stared at the casket. He quivered and choked back a sob. Hesitantly, he stepped toward the box holding his precious son until his outstretched hand touched the polished wood. His chin dropped to his chest, his shoulders shook, and tears streamed down his face.

Mom slipped an arm around his waist and held him until he regained his composure. She guided him gently back to the chairs. They collapsed into the seats.

Dean's girlfriend of the moment came next, dressed in black and wailing like a widow. Her name eluded me. She settled into the vacant chair beside my parents. My chair. There if I wanted it. I resented her for it, even though I stood with the pallbearers.

The enormous crowd of mourners encircled the grave. Most of the high school students—at least, the popular kids— had turned out despite it being the start of summer vacation. Teachers and coaches comforted each other. Stoic farmers— some in suits, some in overalls, and all friends of my dad— stood with their families.

Sarah caught my eye. She and Xander, whom I couldn't find in the horde, were my bandmates and my best friends. My only friends, really.

I looked away from her. I wasn't being fair. We hadn't spoken since the night before the accident. I had returned none of her calls. Seeing her hurt too much after what she had done. She and Dean.

My last conversation with my brother had been a shouting match, a fight in front of everyone in the parking lot of the VFW after the graduation party. The last time I saw him, I was lying in the parking lot, nursing my wounds as he drove away angrily. Our fists had flown because of her.

The murmuring hushed as the minister stepped in front of the casket and spread his arms. "Let us pray."

Heads dropped. Eyes closed. The preacher's booming voice covered the sound of chirping birds as he intoned his prayer. It would be long, his usual style.

I had waited for this moment. Planned it.

Time to act.

For my entire life, I'd been the invisible man, always hidden in the shadow of the great Dean McDougal. No one noticed me at school, at parties, around town, or when a group hung out with Dean at the house. They wouldn't notice me now.

I shuffled backward. The crowd parted to clear a path for me then closed ranks again, hiding me from my parents' view in case they bothered to look, though I knew they wouldn't.

As soon as I reached the periphery of the mob, I turned and ambled across the cemetery, running my fingers along the cold granite of tombstones. As little kids, Dean and I had explored them all after church on Sundays while waiting for our parents. Some dated back to the 1700s. Many of them were McDougals.

Dean had loved the family's century-old ties to Miller County. To him, the names carved in granite were testaments to all that the family had accomplished. To me, each grave marked someone who had failed to escape.

Just another way we were opposites. Dean wanted nothing more than to live his whole life in Miller County. I had been waiting for the freedom of high school graduation so I could flee.

Dean had gotten his wish, though not in the way he had thought. His whole short life had been spent in this place. Then he was buried in this cemetery. Trapped forever.

Not me. I needed to claim my destiny. I had known for years I wouldn't find it in Miller County. It was out there. Somewhere.

The preacher's voice carried across the cemetery. "Ashes to ashes, dust to dust…"

As I pushed open the iron gate exit, the hinges squeaked, but no one looked up. I stepped into the overflowing gravel parking lot. My rusty old Honda Civic—the foreign car Dad hated so much—waited among the minivans, pickup trucks, and Jeeps.

When I reached the car, the preacher's voice fell silent. The whir of gears lowering Dean's coffin assaulted my ears. I slipped inside and shut the door, mercifully blocking out that awful noise.

With trembling hands, I ripped off my tie and threw it into the back seat, on top of the duffel bag stuffed with my clothes. My two guitars rested safely in their cases. My amp was nestled in the corner. Everything I needed was in that car. I cranked the engine and backed through the cloud of blue smoke.

When I reached the road, tears welled up and spilled down my cheeks. I gently pulled off the sunglasses that I had worn throughout the service. I leaned toward the rearview mirror and touched the purple bruise around my eye. The last thing Dean had ever given me.

Nothing was left for me here. I turned my car toward the highway and my freedom.

2

Seventeen years passed before I returned to his grave. The dewy grass soaked the knees of my jeans as I knelt next to the gravestone and traced the raised bronze letters with a quivering finger.

Dean Thomas McDougal
Beloved Son, Brother, and Friend
April 30, 1988–June 4, 2006

I had never seen the marker. If I'd thought about it all, I assumed it simply had his name and the dates of his birth and death. During my sporadic calls home, we had discussed the weather, crops, and church. Surface topics. Things where no feelings got hurt and the expectations were light.

We rarely discussed Dean. Certainly never the accident. The funeral. The grave. Or the epitaph. It all hurt too much.

Had they chosen it before I left? Or did that come later?

Beloved Son

Our parents certainly adored him. The golden boy. The perfect child. Destined to live his life in this godforsaken town. That was what he'd wanted, and they loved him for it. Farm the soil. Go to church. Marry a local girl. Raise an heir. Saddle the next generation with the family farm. When life drew to a close, get buried in this church's cemetery along with the rest of the clan. Just like had happened to McDougals for over two hundred years.

Beloved Friend

Dean's friends had showered him with attention and accolades during his brief life. For as long as I could remember, he'd been at the center of every big event. His athletic prowess was on display as early as T-ball and Pee Wee football. If a group of friends gathered to play in the woods, he was the inventor of the games. On the playground at school, he was always one of the captains doing schoolyard picks.

They still chose me next to last. Only Xander had saved me from the disgrace of being left alone for the last draw.

Just in his last year, he was class president. Homecoming king. Captain of the football team and baseball team. Life of every party. Dater of all the pretty girls.

Beloved Brother

I'm the only person with a valid opinion on that topic. No one ever asked. If they had, I would have told them growing up as Dean's little brother hadn't been a picnic. Always being compared. Always coming up short.

But as frustrating as living in Millerton with Mr. Perfect was, living here without him would have been impossible. I'd never planned to come back.

And I didn't... until my mother called. "Your father is

dying. You need to come say your goodbyes before it's too late."

I pushed myself to my feet and brushed the grass off my black jeans. A gust of wind rolled down the mountains and across the valley floor. The trees at the edge of the empty cemetery offered little protection. My leather jacket creaked as I pulled it tight against my body and shivered.

I'd forgotten how cold a June morning in the North Carolina mountains could be. Despite years dressing for rehearsals on cold stages, I'd somehow failed to throw a sweatshirt into my suitcase. Maybe I'd been in too much of a hurry.

I hadn't been on many stages in the last few years, though, not since Covid shut concerts down. They'd come back, but not for me. We'd had creative differences in my last band. They went in a different direction. That wasn't the first time it had happened to me.

There would be enough time to worry about what to do next once I escaped Millerton's clutches again. For now, though, I would stop in town to get a sweatshirt before going to the house. Besides, clothes shopping, even in the slim pickings of this town, was another good excuse to delay going to the house. I'd stopped at the cemetery to visit Dean's grave for the same reason.

I plodded between the stones, much like I had on that last day. A few new graves were sprinkled about, but most were the same as I remembered. And most were McDougals.

As I neared the big iron gate that led to the parking lot, I paused at a faded, moss-covered stone with roughly carved letters. The day I'd first noticed it remained burned into my memory.

3

The one reliable adventure away from the farm had happened every Sunday—church. The old white clapboard building sat at the end of the gravel road running beside our farm, so it wasn't far. Still, we'd dressed in our cleanest jeans and T-shirts and sworn we would be on our best behavior.

We sat in the same hard pew every week, fighting the urge to squirm lest we feel the rap of knuckles against the back of our skulls, and listened to the preacher's booming voice rail against the sin of the week. If we sat still through the entire service, which was a challenging feat, our reward was to go outside and play while our parents socialized.

At five years old, Dean was still mostly stuck hanging with me. The older kids knew each other from school, something we hadn't yet experienced, and preferred to hang at the far end of the parking lot, away from both parents and little kids like us. We liked it when Russ was there, but the Caldwells didn't come to church every Sunday. "Scandalous," our mother would whisper.

One Sunday, we exited into the summer warmth. As the older kids wandered away and ignored us, Dean announced he had a new game for us to play. Most of the games he invented ended up in me getting hurt by some silly stunt, but this one sounded harmless—whoever found the oldest tombstone in the cemetery won.

"We aren't supposed to play in the cemetery," I protested.

Dean's eyes twinkled. "Freddie's a chicken. Freddie's a chicken."

He'd hurled the ultimate insult, a name he knew hurt me the worst, mostly because it was true. Dean feared nothing, not even punishment. "I'm not, but Mom said—"

"Yep. Chicken."

I threw my bony shoulders back and did my best tough-guy imitation. "I'll do it."

For half a second, I thought I'd surprised him, but a mischievous grin crept across Dean's face. He had, of course, known exactly how to get me to do what he wanted. "What's the bet?"

"Why we gotta bet?"

"What fun is a game if the winner don't get something?"

He would be the winner, of course. "We could play for funsies."

Dean rolled his eyes. "Funsies? You're such a little kid."

Backed into a corner, I retorted with the only thing my five-year-old mind thought of. "Am not."

"Then bet."

I blurted out the first idea that popped into my head. "Loser does the winner's chores after church."

Dean's grin became a full-fledged smile, showing off the gap where he had lost his first two baby teeth—months before me, of course. He offered his hand to seal the bet. "Deal."

My stomach sank, but it was too late to back out. I would

be stuck doing whatever nasty task he was supposed to do out in the barn. And I would still have to do my normal chores—sweep off the front porch, pick up the branches in the yard, and weed Mom's flower gardens.

We shook hands. I raced from grave to grave, checking the dates on the markers. I ignored the newer bronze plaques and shiny granite stones. The older stones, however, offered promise. World War II. World War I. Then the 1900s blended into the 1800s. A large cluster marked the Civil War era. After that, the dates became harder and harder to read on the faded stones.

One name, however, appeared over and over. McDougals stretched back over the decades and centuries. Until that day, I had never pondered how our family had come to this remote valley.

I looked for Dean to ask. Rather than sweating or racing about, he was sitting on the ground beside a stone near the picket-fence gate to the parking lot. His face beamed with amusement and confidence. I knew I'd been beaten. Again. Dean always won.

Dejected, I dragged my feet over to him and studied the stone behind his back.

Hobard Samuel McDougal
February 21, 1763–November 23, 1791

"Who is that?"

Dean lay back and stared into the sky. "The first McDougal."

"First ever?"

He snorted and slipped a blade of grass into his mouth, letting the stalk hang out in a mirror image of Dad. "No, silly, the first one here."

Mesmerized, I gazed at the stone. "Where did he come from?"

"Ireland."

"How did he get here?"

"Boat."

I waved my arm at the surrounding mountains. "How?"

"A boat to America, stupid. He walked or rode a horse or something to here."

Despite the sting of defeat, that was, I had to admit, pretty cool. "How do you know he's the first?"

"Dad told me. Hobard was supposed to live with some cousins in Philadelphia or Pittsburgh or something, but it was too crowded, and people didn't like Irish back then."

"Why not?"

"Don't know. Just didn't."

"That's stupid."

Dean shrugged it off. "So he kept looking for a place to call home and followed the mountains all the way down until he came into this valley. Wide-open land. No one here. Perfect for farming."

It wasn't until years later that I learned the Cherokee were here before our family. Ultimately, most of them were driven out of the area. On the day I'd learned about Hobard, though, I hadn't known any of that. "So he's, like, our great-grandpa?"

"Great-great-great-great..." Dean's face scrunched in thought. "I don't know how many greats, but Dad told me lots."

When I was sick, Dean hung out in the barn with Dad so Mom could look after me. It wasn't Dean's fault, but I was still always jealous of all the stories Dad told him. Dean, of course, knew that, so he shared the stories to bug me, just like he snuck animals into my room to scare me.

But him telling me all these details also explained something else. "So, you knew he was buried here 'cause Dad told you?"

"Yeah."

"And you knew he was the oldest?"

"Yeah."

"So you cheated."

Dean sat up and glared. "Did not."

"But you knew."

"Didn't say I didn't."

"That's cheating."

"No, it's not."

"I'm not doing your chores."

"Yeah, you are. You shook on it."

"Don't count 'cause you cheated, cheater."

Dean stood up and balled his fist. "Take that back."

"Cheater. Cheater. Cheater. Cheater."

Dean shoved me. It wasn't the first fight we'd ever had, not by a long shot, but it was the first at church.

All these years later, I still felt the sting of tears rolling down my face, mixed with the blood dripping from my nose, as our dad held his sons apart with his powerful grip on our shirt collars.

I ran my fingers along the top of Hobard's stone. The fight was as clear in my mind as if it had happened yesterday. That was the way Millerton was—the ghosts of the past always haunting. Hobard Samuel demanded thanks over the centuries for bringing the McDougals here.

What haunted me the most about that day wasn't Dean's cheating. Or the inevitable fight that broke out. Or even Dean's grin and triumphant laugh. He didn't care about the bet, chores, the coming punishment, or even Hobard. All he cared about was winning. Beating me.

What galled me was what happened when we got home from church. Dean's punishment was cleaning out the barn, a task he liked to complain about but really enjoyed. He was outdoors, doing physical work, and sweating. Even at the ripe age of five, he already liked that stuff.

Me? My punishment was doing Dean's original chores that day, in addition to my own. To pay off the bet. To let Dean win.

"A deal's a deal," Dad said.

4

Beckett's Feed and Seed looked the same as it always had —another time warp from my growing-up years in Millerton. A tall chain-link fence encircled a sprawling gravel parking lot. Tractors for sale, both new and used, were parked along the front beside rows of farm implements. Stacks of various sizes of pipes—both PVC and concrete—and rolls of wire fencing lined the rear.

A long building stretched through the center of the property. The bulk of the building was an open warehouse stacked with seed, fertilizer, hay, and feed. Workers scurried about, loading supplies into pickups and flatbed trucks backed up to a dock. Men in overalls, jeans, flannel shirts, and muddy work boots clustered in groups as they swapped town news and tall tales.

The part of the building closest to the lot's entrance was my target. Enclosed with plate-glass windows, the store housed supplies for household cleaning, pets, and other basic needs for farming families. For clothing that was more about durability than fashion, Beckett's was the place.

In the rare years of abundant harvests, Dean and I

received new clothes. Not just new-to-us clothes from the church bazaar or Goodwill. In those good times, we were allowed to buy never-worn-by-anyone-else clothes. We would take off half a day on a Saturday, an uncommon break from farm chores, and go shopping.

Not to Asheville, of course. Our old man had an expressed opinion of how dirty, dangerous, and sinful things were down there. Of course, as we became teens, that only made the city more attractive to us. But as kids, we were stuck with Beckett's. Dad said everything a man ever needed could come from there.

That was true enough, if that man was a farmer. Dean and Dad were as happy as pigs in mud, flipping through racks of Carhartt jeans, flannel shirts, and work boots.

I wanted more, but I was smart enough not to complain. New was better than Dean's old stuff. At least new didn't stink of sweat and grime. "Beggars can't be choosers," Mom always said.

And that was true now too. I needed a sweatshirt. As tempting as it was to spend a couple of hours driving down to Asheville to find an actual store, I needed to eventually see my parents. I knew I could only delay for so long.

I parked among the smattering of cars near the entrance and got out of the SUV. My foot no sooner touched gravel than heads swiveled in my direction and people gawked.

When I had landed at the Charlotte airport a few hours earlier, a nondescript beige sedan awaited me in the rental lot. A shiny black Escalade—exactly what a successful, rich rock star would drive—had sat a few rows over. For my triumphant return after leaving Millerton seeking fame and fortune, I needed to look like I had achieved it.

Standing in the parking lot of Beckett's, though, I regretted my impulse. Among the Jeeps, trucks, sedans, and minivans, a big SUV with tinted windows stood out. The people staring weren't thinking of a celebrity. The vehicle screamed lost tourist or, worse, one of those part-year residents who summered in those monster homes perched high in the mountains.

And if the car didn't attract enough attention, my long hair, tattooed body, and black clothing would. I felt their eyes crawling over me.

From some distant memory, Dad's voice came to me. "When you're going through hell, march straight through." I threw my shoulders back, straightened up, and walked confidently toward the front door. Let them think whatever they wanted. I had nothing to prove.

Besides, I'd been gone for seventeen years. No one would recognize me.

A group of men, all focused on me, huddled beside a mudsplattered farm truck. I probably knew them all, if I hadn't blocked them from my memories, but one stood out and made my heart skip a beat. He leaned back against the side of the vehicle, one leg cocked and the sole of his work boot resting on the tire. A tight-fitting T-shirt advertising beer stretched across his broad chest and even-broader belly. His sunburned, hairy arms were thick, his hands stuffed in his pants pockets. A day's worth of stubble grew on his cheek, puffed out from a wad of tobacco. A worn brown ball cap was pulled tightly over his head.

Despite the toll the years had taken on him, I knew Blake Torrence at a glance. He had been proud of his muscles and liked to use his strength on littler kids like me. He'd always seemed to have a cut or bruise from scuffles. I'd done my best to avoid him, but that was difficult since he was one of Dean's close friends ever since he and Dean had come to blows back in the first grade.

Dean could throw a punch and was fearless when a fight broke out. On the football field. On the basketball court. Even in a dugout-clearing brawl on the baseball diamond. And, as he'd proven in that church cemetery, with his little brother who'd dared to call him a cheater.

But unlike Blake, Dean usually didn't start the fights. He enjoyed making friends more than enemies.

From the time we were six and boarded the brightly colored school bus for the first time for the long ride into town and the county schools, Dean had made friends fast. He'd been the clown in the classroom, making others laugh. On the sports fields, he'd been the star who made everyone stare in awe.

Me? I'd preferred the back row of desks so the teacher wouldn't call on me. I knew the answers, but I didn't want to bring attention to myself. During recess, I blamed my allergies and snuck off with a book to avoid the scrum of sports on the playground. My discovery of the school library made my solitude a heaven. By isolating myself, though, I made for easy prey.

One day, as recess began, the rest of the class filed outside, and I made my escape down a hallway. Thinking I'd gone unnoticed, I got halfway to the library before I heard the squeak of tennis shoes approaching. Blake and two of his pals had followed. I looked for Dean to come to my rescue, but he'd gone outside to play. I was alone with the trio, each bigger and stronger than me.

I tried to run, but their hands were on me before I made it far. They flung me against the wall, knocking my breath out of me. Two of them pinned my arms, leaving me face-to-face with Blake. He jabbed a finger into my rib cage and demanded my lunch money.

Without Dean, I was helpless. The tears flowed easily and rolled down my cheeks. I felt the spreading warmth of my pee soaking the crotch of my pants. I put up no resistance.

One little goon let my hand go free long enough for me to pull my cash from my pocket and hold it out with my shaking hand. Blake laughed, snatched the coins, and punched me in the stomach. They left me on the floor, crumpled and humiliated. As I lay there sobbing, all I thought was that at least Dad hadn't witnessed my cowardice.

When lunch rolled around, I sat alone at a table, friendless and without food. Dean, surrounded by his buddies, saw me. He came over and demanded to know where my lunch was. My answer infuriated him. No one messed with a McDougal— not even the scrawniest member—without risking retaliation.

Dean didn't hesitate. He balled his hands into fists and marched across the cafeteria to the table where Blake and his pals sat. I expected him to demand the money back, get into an argument, and maybe escalate the situation into a fight, but Dean was in no mood to talk. He wasted no words. He slugged Blake without warning.

The other two boys came to Blake's defense, and the fight turned into a three-against-one brawl. Despite being outnumbered, Dean held his own. He didn't exactly win, but he didn't lose either. By the time the teachers broke it up, all four boys were bloodied and bruised.

About an hour later, Dean returned from the principal's office. He sported a nice shiner but was grinning triumphantly. He slapped my money down on my desk without saying a word. Then he turned and sat down with his new pals—Blake and company. They'd bonded while waiting for their punishment.

I resented that he could be nice to the guys who had bullied me, but at least it was over. Or so I thought. The worst came later.

When Dean and I stepped off the bus the afternoon of the fight, Mom took one look at his bruised face and knuckles and demanded to know what had happened. When the story was finished, Dad turned to me, lifted my hands, and examined them for marks. Seeing none, he said, "You gotta stand up for yourself, son. Dean ain't always going to be there to protect you. If you defend yourself, they'll leave you alone."

He might have been right, though I wasn't sure Blake would've broken a sweat if I had fought back. It wasn't my fault I wasn't big, tough, and brave like Dean. I wanted Dad to see that, but he was too busy tending to Dean's injuries. He pulled a bandanna out of his back pocket, wrapped it around a few cubes of ice, and gently touched it against Dean's black eye.

Dad's next question hung in the air ever since that day. "Why can't you be more like your brother?"

I'd like to say I took my father's words, no matter how hurtful, to heart and learned to stand up for myself. That would be a lie, though.

Blake and company had promised Dean they would leave me alone. They kept their promise and never picked on me again. But that protection didn't extend to everyone. Blake was merciless to anyone smaller and weaker, and that included the few friends I'd had growing up.

In a way, that was worse. He would confront them right in front of me. I couldn't do a thing when he pushed them, ridiculed them, or humiliated them. I watched the tears well up in their eyes and could never take away their hurt.

I'd hated him for it then. Seeing him again caused those memories to bubble up inside me. The hate seethed through my body. I no more wanted to deal with Blake Torrence as an adult than I had as a piss-soaked six-year-old.

So when Blake's expression changed in that parking lot, when the glimmer of recognition flickered through his eyes, and when he pushed himself off that truck and moved toward me, my name on his lips, I did what I do best. I got back in my garish SUV and drove away.

5

O nce Beckett's dwindled to a receding dot in my rearview mirror, I pounded the dash in frustration. Coming back to Millerton was a mistake. Too many Blakes tormented me in this place. People didn't change. They couldn't. Once a bully, always a bully.

But as Dad had tried to teach me while tending to Dean's wounds, I couldn't let the Blakes of the world dictate my life. I wasn't like Dean. I wasn't brave enough to confront Blake, but I could avoid him for a few days. Avoidance was one skill I had mastered.

I'd come this far. I would drive to the safety of my old home and stay there for as long as I needed. When things were done, I could drive back to Charlotte and catch the first available flight. Get back to my real life. Back to being Mad Maverick McDougal, rock star. Or whatever it was I'd become.

I might not have ever achieved the superstardom I'd fantasized about as a kid, but at least out there on the road was better than living here, where I was nothing more than Freddie McDougal, little brother of Dean, Little Mac to the Big Mac.

Fighting back tears, I gripped the steering wheel until my

knuckles turned white. *Little Mac. How do I let these things haunt me all these years later?*

The quickest route to my childhood home took me through the familiar streets of the center of Millerton. In the distant past, the three downtown blocks had bustled with activity, though that was long before I was born. Half the storefronts had been vacant when I was a kid.

Things had only grown worse since. If it weren't for the county government building—complete with the sheriff's department and volunteer fire department—on one end and Sammy's Pub on the other, little would be happening.

Halfway through the center block, a hand-painted sign on a window caught my eye—Stewart's Consignments. A pair of glass doors was propped open, inviting passersby inside, not that any pedestrians were in sight.

I slowed and peered through the doors. The store had been one of my few refuges when I was a teenager. It had served as the rehearsal space for the Wicked Centipedes.

If anyone was more of an outcast than me at school, it was Xander Stewart. I, at least, had Dean as a protector, even if he was only interested in the family name. Xander had nobody, so Blake and his minions made his life hell. I hated it, but it was better than me being the target.

Geeky, quiet, and prone to tell weird jokes, he was always out of step. That quirkiness made us the best of friends. We bonded over our lowly status.

Plus, we shared a love of music. For most kids in Millerton, the music selection was limited to what played on the Asheville radio stations. Cell phones hadn't become widespread, and only a lucky few had home access to the internet. Streaming music was beyond comprehension.

But we had a secret weapon—Anna Stewart, Xander's mother, and her consignment store. In addition to an assortment of used clothes, furniture, and books, she carried an eclectic collection of records and tapes. She let us pick over the selection and take things into the back of the store to listen on an old stereo.

One day, when someone brought in a drum set to sell, Xander begged, and Anna bought it for him. He hauled it into the back of the store and taught himself to play. I did the same with a used guitar, which I paid for by hauling furniture around the store. We imitated the songs we listened to, playing for hours in our hideaway, dreaming of being rock stars.

I'd never thanked her for giving us a safe space. The Blakes of our little world couldn't touch us there while we learned about music of all types. And I ate almost as many meals at her kitchen table as I did at home.

If one good thing could come from this miserable trip, seeing Anna Stewart would be it. Plus, she could tell me where Xander was living. It would be good to catch up with my old friend. Besides, I still needed a sweatshirt. It was as good an excuse to stop as any.

I parked in one of the many empty parallel parking spaces in front of the store and went inside. An electronic chime announced my arrival. No customers were in the store browsing the rows of merchandise, but it looked the same. Used furniture cluttered the center. Aisles of knickknacks and racks of clothes took up the rest of the floor space. Shelves of books, records, CDs, and DVDs lined one wall. The other wall had always been my favorite—used musical instruments.

In the center of the back wall, a curtain covered the entrance to the storage area. A muffled voice—a man's, not Anna's—floated from beyond. "Feel free to look around. I'll be right out. Trying to grab my lunch real quick."

Maybe they'd sold the business but left the name on it. I still needed a hoodie, so I flipped through the racks until I found what I wanted. Solid black. No logos. No stains. A reasonable amount of wear.

With my mission accomplished and my purchase in hand, I scanned the store while I waited at the cash register. An acoustic guitar hanging on the wall grabbed my attention and drew me across the store. A quick strum brought a grimace to my face, but I tuned it quickly enough. The neck and frets were in decent shape, though it needed new strings. It didn't sound the greatest but was far better than the one I'd learned to play on.

Ever since I was a kid, the magic of music had mesmerized me. As an adult, I felt no different. My fingers moved, my toes tapped, and I lost myself in the melody. The world and my problems faded away as they always did. I never heard the man emerge from the back, so I was surprised when I looked up. He was standing frozen, a napkin in his hand, a smear of errant mustard on a cheek.

As soon as we made eye contact, a smile broke across his face. "Holy moly, is that really Freddie McDougal, the legendary guitarist of the Wicked Centipedes?"

A sense of buoyancy hit me for the first time since the phone call the day before. Xander's long hair had been cropped close and was peppered with premature gray. A bit of a beer belly betrayed his wiry frame. A day's stubble covered the formerly smooth cheeks. Glasses perched on his nose fixed his perpetual squint. Despite the changes, I knew my old best friend at a glance.

I embraced him. "Didn't know you would be here. I stopped to ask your mom how to get in touch with you."

"She passed a few years ago." Xander glanced down at the floor but just as quickly looked up and spread his arms wide. "I'm the king of the Stewart retail empire now."

After I offered my condolences and we chatted about her for a few minutes, I asked, "You still playing? Have your drums in the back?"

"Yeah, but I don't play much anymore. The Wicked

Centipedes was my last band. When you disappeared without telling anyone, including me"—Xander narrowed his eyes—"there wasn't much of a band left."

I avoided his glare. "You and Sarah. You could've found another guitar."

"Sarah? She never really wanted much to do with me. Barely talked to me after the funeral."

Even all these years later, I heard the heartbreak lingering in his voice. He had been in love with her for as long as I could remember. His infatuation made things awkward between us from the first day we saw her because I fell for her too. We used to laugh about it with each other, pretending we would compete for her affection. We both knew it didn't matter, because neither of us stood a chance with her. Half the guys in our class felt the same way. Probably all of them.

Whenever she went on a date with one of them, Xander became despondent. He agonized over whether he'd lost her, even though he'd never worked up the guts to tell her how he felt.

Still, it surprised me to hear the pain in his voice after all these years as he looked up at the ceiling and said, "Next thing I knew, she married Russ Caldwell."

Sarah was one of those people who could easily float from one clique to another in high school without upsetting the social rules. She simply didn't think the rules should exist, so she ignored them. She could hang with Xander and me, the geekiest of the geeks, without damaging her reputation one iota. She'd just as easily spent time with Dean and the popular kids without letting it go to her head.

When I'd heard she married Russ, I was surprised because I'd never known them to date. More, though, it shocked me because she had always said she was leaving Millerton. It was one of the things we shared. She wasn't from here. I didn't want to be.

But I'd never heard why she married him. Xander shrugged. "Oldest Millerton story in the book. She got preggers. Just whispers, of course, but they eloped in the fall and the kid was born before spring, so you do the math."

I didn't want to talk about that. Maybe I still had some lingering feelings myself. "You could've formed a band with some of those guys down in Asheville."

"They were your friends, not mine." When I tried to protest, he cut me off. "Didn't matter, because Mom got sick the fall after you pulled your disappearing act. I had to keep this place running."

I hadn't known and tried to explain, but my clumsy explanation sounded weak. The only people I spoke to from Millerton after I left were my parents. My mother's opinion that Xander was an "odd duck" must have prevented her from sharing the news.

Xander waved off my apologies and motioned me through the curtains to the rear of the store. I turned to hang the guitar back on the wall, but he told me to bring it on back. Maybe we could play for old times' sake, he suggested.

When I came through the curtains, I realized how little the place had changed. Stacked boxes waited to be unpacked alongside old furniture in various stages of repair before hitting the sales floor. The scent of wood stain mingled with the damp, mildewy odor of warehouse space. The chilly air made me shiver. I warmed myself with the space heater beside Anna's old desk pushed up against a cinderblock wall.

On the wall hung a series of pictures of Xander growing up, mostly annual school photos. Anna had proudly added one each year. Beside them, she—or maybe Xander—had added his high school diploma. A cheap chain draped over one corner of the frame held a dangling Millerton High School class ring. The gold was dented but polished. Tucked to the side of Xander's wall of honor was a photo of Anna's old Camaro, a car we both coveted, parked in their driveway.

A collage of photos of the Wicked Centipedes drew my focus. Some were taken when just Xander and I were practicing in this warehouse. Later ones included Sarah. I'd seen most of them before, but not the ones of our final show. The best night of my life. Before Dean got himself killed the next morning.

Xander followed my eyes to the photos and smiled. "Those were the days."

He went into the back corner of the warehouse space—our old rehearsal hall—and dusted off what remained of his drum set. He motioned me to my old stool still bearing my carved initials.

Our music was rusty and disjointed. I'd never stopped playing, and he had. We hadn't jammed together in seventeen years, not since that fateful night.

Despite the cobwebs and the sporadic interruptions from the occasional customer, the next couple of hours were the best I'd had in months. Maybe even years. Music didn't always have to be good to be rewarding. *What's a few sour notes between friends?*

6

Asheville was the forbidden city. Dad would tsk as we sat in the front parlor, watching the TV news blast images of crime scenes. On Sundays, the preacher railed about temptation and sin, most of which seemed to come from our big-city neighbor, according to his sermons.

As kids, we only ever went there with my father for specific errands for the farm. He drove white-knuckled and ranting about the crazy drivers. Cars whipped past our old truck like we were on a racetrack. They would honk as we puttered along, hauling hay or tractor parts.

When I was sixteen, Anna gave me the first taste of how magical the place could be. One summer Sunday when the store was closed, Xander and I squeezed into her Camaro and took off to a street festival in downtown Asheville. Not just in sin city but the heart of sin city. I couldn't have been more excited.

And since we didn't have school, I was staying the night at Xander's. That saved me from having to tell my parents where we were going. They assumed Xander and I were playing music in the back of the consignment store.

Once we finally found a place to park, blocks from the event, we walked along the sidewalk, chattering excitedly. The distant music echoed off the buildings, muffled by the din of the mob of people moving in our same direction.

The smell of food hung in the air, tempting me the same way our county fair did every fall, but it wasn't mingled with the scent of livestock. This was city life.

We walked past the street barricades and entered a sea of tents lining the sidewalks. Vendors displayed their wares. Paintings. Sculptures. Jewelry. Clothing. Most of it was ridiculously expensive, far more than I could afford with the measly few dollars in my pocket, but tourists snatched the stuff up.

When we arrived at a park near the center of the city, we settled onto the grass and listened to music played on a giant stage. People danced in the crowd. Anna brought us wraps and drinks from a street vendor as we sat, mesmerized listening to real live stars. Not superstars, of course, but people who had cut an actual record. We had only listened to them in the back of Anna's store, and now we were watching them in the flesh.

On the Friday and Saturday, the festival had run into the evening, but it closed at five o'clock on Sunday. When the festival ended, we were still buzzing from the excitement. Anna led us on an excursion through the downtown area. Loud music poured out of bars. People sat at tables on sidewalks in front of restaurants, eating fancy food and drinking wine and beer.

We walked up and down hills through the maze of twisting streets. Mesmerized by the crowds and the sights and sounds, I would never have found my way back to the car on my own.

We came upon a small open area with an eight-feet-tall sculpture at its center—an iron set on its heel like it was waiting to press the wrinkles out of a shirt. A man painted all in silver like a statue came alive to surprise tourists walking past. A magician impressed a small crowd with card tricks. He bantered with them, a string of cheesy jokes that made everyone laugh.

Sitting on a chair in the center of a sizable audience was a man playing a guitar. He was singing and cutting up with them as they tossed money into his guitar case. When we approached, he smiled and winked at Anna.

After he finished his set and bowed to appreciative applause, he crossed to us and hugged Anna. "Darling," he crowed, "so glad you called. I haven't seen you in ages." He drew out his words comically.

"Charlie, you remember my son, don't you?"

"No way he can be yours. You're too young to have a kid this old!"

She blushed and pointed at me. "And this is Freddie, the young man I told you about."

He bowed before me with theatrical exaggeration. "Always a pleasure to meet a fellow musician. Anna tells me you are fabulous." With his loud emphasis on each syllable of that last word, he had the people milling about laughing.

I felt my face turn red.

He grabbed my arm and pulled me toward the chair and his waiting guitar. "Do you have a song prepared?"

"A what?"

"A song, honey. You're about to be on stage."

"No, wait. I can't—"

He ignored my protests and clapped his hands for attention. "Ladies and gentlemen, I give you the world premiere of Freddie McDonald!"

"Dougal."

He leaned over to hear me. "Huh?"

"McDougal. It's McDougal."

"It's McMud if you don't entertain them, so sit your butt down in that chair and play."

I looked to Anna for help, but she was cheering along with

everyone else. She knew me well enough to know that I would have refused to go to Asheville with her if I had known what she was planning. No way was I playing in front of strangers. Except now, I was stuck. My choice was to run or make some music. And if I ran, I didn't know how to get home. I could never face Anna after chickening out, even if I found them again.

With my heart racing, I picked up his guitar, settled into the seat, and tried to think of what to play. My fingers fumbled over the strings, and sweat rolled down my forehead.

Charlie leaned over and whispered to me, "Just relax and have fun. The crowd wants to have a good time. As long as you give them that, you're gold."

I closed my eyes, took a deep breath, and began picking the strings, hesitantly at first. But then the music settled over me. The crowd faded from my mind. The notes slipped out. I was falling into the trance that let me play.

Chink.

I opened an eye, surprised to see a quarter rolling in Charlie's guitar case. My first payment as a professional musician. I wished I'd saved it, but it blended with the money already there.

Inspired by the falling coin, the song floated through me. A couple danced on the sidewalk. A group of college kids swayed to the beat. A dollar bill floated out of a man's hand and into the case. My spirits soared. I was playing guitar and getting paid for it.

When I finished the first song, the crowd applauded politely. Charlie whispered another song into my ear and asked if I knew it. I started picking the notes. To my surprise, his voice belted out, singing the lyrics as I played. The crowd roared its approval as he clowned with them. Money dribbled into the case.

Charlie grabbed Anna's hand, and they danced on the

sidewalk, singing along with my playing. Xander beat the percussion rhythm against a plastic bucket. A police officer stood on the sidewalk, tapping his toe, a smile on his face. I saw a five-dollar bill get added to the pot.

I was hooked and could have played all night. After the set, though, Charlie stopped simply by announcing that I would play one last song. I did. The crowd cheered, money got tossed, and another musician moved to the chair.

We perched on a ledge and listened. Charlie explained they shared the corner, mapping out a schedule of who played when. They also kept a watch over each other, protecting as needed and cheering successes. And, importantly, their constant playing kept others from poaching their prime spot. To my surprise, he gave me his phone number and invited me to come play with them. He introduced me around so that they knew I was a welcome part of the crew.

In those early days, my busking time was limited because I always needed a ride to get there. I couldn't ask my parents. I didn't want to tell Dean. Xander, when he could borrow the Camaro, came with me. A few times, I hitched rides. I saved every penny until I scraped together enough money to buy an ancient Honda Civic.

Dad hated that thing. I should have bought American, he said. And he asked where I'd gotten the money.

I couldn't tell him, though. Not earning it in Asheville. Certainly not playing music for money. I knew without even saying it that he considered that begging. I couldn't sully the McDougal name like that.

So I told him I'd earned it working for Anna. He looked unsure, but he never asked again. Maybe he just didn't want to know.

But he was right about the car. It was a clunker. Fortunately, Dean helped me with it. He fixed it up so it wouldn't break down going back and forth on Interstate 40, though

Dean thought I was just driving it around Millerton, mostly to and from Xander's. I tried to pay him, but he refused to take anything except for the price of the parts.

All I cared about was that I was playing music. Getting cheers from audiences. Getting paid for it all. And making friends who were as about music as I was.

7

W hen Xander and I put down our instruments and agreed to meet again the next day to jam, I left relaxed and ready to finally go home. It was early afternoon, hours after my intended arrival, when I made my way well outside of town and turned off the pavement onto the old familiar gravel road.

The Caldwell farm sat on the right. The McDougal land was to the left. Rows of corn stretched in either direction until they reached the foot of the mountains. Dust rose behind my vehicle, blocking the last remnants of modern civilization from view.

The few gravel roads I had been on in the last several years were rough and rutted, but not this one. It was smooth and maintained. Every other spring, we would drag this road to eliminate the washboard that formed over the winter and to add gravel to thin spots. In the opposite years, the Caldwells handled the task. The few families that lived farther up in the mountains never helped. We had the equipment, and they didn't. Simple enough.

Is it the Caldwells' year? If Dad was so sick, he couldn't have been able to operate a box blade on a tractor. *But he couldn't have planted the acres of corn either. Did they hire someone to help?* Hiring seasonal help was one thing. We'd done it out of necessity at certain times of year, but someone had to be out in the fields every day.

The tires crossed from the gravel to the old wooden bridge over the creek Dean and I had played in as kids. The hum of the tires over the boards changed back to the crunch of gravel, the sign to look for the mailbox marking the entrance to our home. With sweaty palms and a churning in my stomach, I turned the SUV into the narrow passage through the corn that was our driveway. The roof of the house peeked over the stalks.

With a suddenness that took my breath away—the same as it had when I was a child—the corn opened to reveal the small yard surrounding our house. The massive maple tree in the front yard stood sentry as it had for a century. The old barn rose behind the house.

The house itself sat in the center of the clearing. Its covered front porch stretched from one corner of the house to the other. It looked the same as it always had. I suspected the interior was also the same.

Three windows on the second floor above the porch marked my bedroom on one side, Dean's on the other, and the small bathroom we shared in between. Our great-grandfather had added it a hundred years earlier when indoor plumbing became a reality.

If we snuck in or out of the house at night, we didn't dare use the steps in the house's interior. Our parents' bedroom was in the rear of the second floor, and they would always hear us coming or going. Instead, we would use our windows, cross the porch roof, and drop to the ground. To return, we climbed the porch supports.

Downstairs, the front parlor was under Dean's room. The

dining room was below mine. The front door in between stood open to let the mountain breezes slip through the screen. The rear parlor, which had been converted to the farm office, and kitchen were toward the back of the house.

I could see every inch clearly in my mind—every piece of furniture, the scuff marks we had left on the floor, and even the colors in each room. I suspected they looked the same as they had the day I'd left.

Somewhere inside, my father lay dying. My mother, I had no doubt, stood in those shadows and watched me through one of the open windows. She would have heard me coming down the gravel from a mile away. We'd always known when a visitor was arriving.

I took a deep breath. After all these years, I was home.

AFTER PARKING in the shade of the sprawling maple tree, I waited to see if she would emerge. When she didn't, I got out and looked around, not wanting to rush inside.

My original impression that nothing had changed was wrong. The longer I stared, the more I noticed. The barn, always neat and orderly in my youth, sagged to one side. No interior lights blazed, so the propped-open door revealed only gloomy shadows. From what little I could see, no bales of hay were stacked inside.

A tractor was parked just in front of the barn in its usual spot beside a row of implements. Rather than looking oiled and fit, the equipment was faded, and rust spots were apparent. Tall grass grew through the openings, a sure sign nothing had moved this spring. One front tire was half-deflated, a sin that would never have been allowed in my youth.

The garden between the house and barn was half-planted. Overgrown weeds strangled what young plants had emerged.

Broken branches lay scattered under the tree. One of my daily chores had been to pick up and dispose of any debris on the lawn.

Only a scar in the bark of the thick branch above my head remained to mark where the tire swing had once hung. I'd loved sitting in that tire with a book in my hand, reading away my summer days. Dean had preferred seeing how high he could swing then leaping from the tire at its peak.

The flower beds surrounding the front steps contained early-spring blooms, but weeds had erupted around them. Mom loved those beds and wanted them perfect. While Dean toiled away in the fields, I'd spent many a day on hands and knees, pulling unwanted growth until my sneezing drove me indoors.

The house needed a fresh coat of paint. A shutter hung from a second-floor window. A gutter had pulled loose from one corner.

All the maintenance work of the house, in addition to running the farm, would have fallen on Dad's shoulders with both Dean and me gone. In my haste to escape, I'd never thought much about how he would manage alone. He had done it before we came, but he was younger then.

That made me wonder again how the fields surrounding the house were so well maintained. Had they hired someone to run the farm? But wouldn't they use the barn and tractor? Maybe a neighboring farmer was leasing the land.

The squeak of the screen door interrupted my thoughts. My mother stepped onto the broad porch and let the door slam closed behind her. She wiped her hands on her apron and stood staring at me.

Her hair was grayer. Wrinkles crisscrossed her face. Age spots dotted the backs of her hands. She looked older than her years, but farming life was hard.

Our sporadic phone calls may have let us hear voices, but

we hadn't seen each other since I'd left. She was sizing me up the same way I was her. The years had changed me too.

My hair might have been too shaggy when I left—a constant battle with the old man about the need to keep it cut —but now it reached well past my shoulders.

The sweatshirt mercifully hid most of my tattoos, but the ink was visible on the backs of my hands. The tattoos Dean and I got on our eighteenth birthdays—a day apart, of course —had caused a massive fight in the house. Why would we want to deface our bodies? My transgression had since gone far beyond that first innocent treble clef inked on my calf.

While we were growing up, Mom hated to see us wear black T-shirts with our jeans. "You look like hoodlums," she would scold. Now I stood in front of her with a black sweatshirt, jeans, and boots, wearing her hated color from head to toe.

With a deep breath, I crossed the yard and climbed the steps like a little boy going to Mommy for his punishment. I braced for a scolding. A tense conversation. Even just a soft tsking.

But she did the last thing I expected. She wrapped her arms around me, pulled me close in a bear hug, and cried.

8

W e sat in the rocking chairs on the front porch. The table between us held a tray of sandwiches and a pitcher of sweet iced tea. My protests that I needed nothing had been ignored, and I was thankful. The scant food I had eaten on the red-eye flight the night before had long stopped satisfying my hunger.

We rocked in silence and watched a hawk soar through the air, floating on the thermals and hunting for its next meal. It circled then dove with astounding speed, disappearing behind the corn for a few seconds. It reemerged with a vole wriggling in its claws.

The corn. Rows and rows of healthy corn. I had to broach the subject. "Who's running the farm?"

Mom's chair squeaked. "Russ Caldwell."

"Russ? Not his daddy?"

"Vern died a few years back. Heart attack out in the field. They didn't find him until he didn't show up for supper."

"That's awful."

"It's the way your daddy always wanted to go. Better than this."

I couldn't deny that, but I wasn't ready for that conversation. I avoided it. "And Russ has the time to tend your fields too?"

"He's done well. Grown his business enough to hire a couple of fellows full-time."

I could sense she had more to say as she rocked back and forth, but I knew better than to rush it. When we were in trouble for some transgression and waiting for the punishment, Dean and I joked that we knew the seriousness of a conversation based on how long it took to get there. Her rocking told me I wouldn't like the answer. My patience was rewarded when she dropped the bomb. "It's not our fields. It's his."

That news took a few minutes to process. This land had belonged to McDougals since old Hobard crossed into the valley. I never had the affinity for it, but I'd never imagined it ever being in anyone else's hands.

She answered the question I couldn't bring myself to ask. "When your daddy got sick, we knew we couldn't handle the farm anymore. Russ offered us a fair price so we could pay off the mortgage, cover his doctor bills, and still have a little left over."

"And the house? Did he buy it too?"

"House goes with the land, but the deal is I get to stay in the house until… well, until I don't need it no more. We did it all legal. Had the lawyer put it in the papers."

Dad would have made sure she was protected. He'd loved the phrase *trust but verify* ever since he heard Reagan utter those words.

We rocked some more, giving me time to think. In city life, people had to pounce to stay in a conversation. I'd forgotten how long a discussion could take out here. "I'm just surprised."

"Shouldn't be. What else were we going to do with it? With Dean gone, no one was left to run it." She grabbed my wrist. "And don't pretend you wanted it. You never did."

"It's not like I hated it."

She tsked. "I didn't say that, but you weren't a farmer. Never wanted to be."

I wanted to protest because it felt like an accusation, not a statement. Still, she was right. I didn't know what I would have done with the land if I'd inherited it. When times were tight, farmers borrowed against the land to stay afloat, so it wouldn't have been unencumbered. I would probably have lost it to the bank trying to keep up with payments.

"Besides," she continued, "this way, it stays a farm, not some housing development or mobile home park."

We rocked and listened to the songbirds. "That had to break Dad's heart. He loved the farm more than anything."

She stopped her chair and turned to look at me. "Not more than you boys."

I couldn't help but roll my eyes. "He loved Dean."

"He loved you both. Only difference is he saw Dean taking over this place. We both knew you were leaving."

"I had to."

She clucked under her breath. "I know."

We sat side by side as time ticked by the way it always did in the country—slowly. I listened to the sound of the rustling corn, the creaking tree branches, and the calling birds. Once the kitchen was cleaned each night, she spent the rest of the evening out here relaxing. She'd never been one for TV. "So you'll be okay living in this big house by yourself?"

"For now. Russ checks in on me regular. Sarah comes by once or twice a week. Their oldest boy mows the lawn. He isn't much about weeding the flowers like you were, but I'll have time to tend to things once your dad is… gone."

We rocked some more. I wanted to ask about Dad, but I didn't want to at the same time. It was my standard tactic of avoidance, but I couldn't force myself to the uncomfortable topic. As she often did, Mom saved me the trouble. "I need to warn you before you see your dad. The cancer… it hasn't been kind. He may be awake. May not. But even if he is, his mind ain't always right. Sometimes he's right there, but sometimes he's far away. And later in the day is always worse than mornings, so don't expect much today."

I swallowed hard and nodded.

"Most, though, the big man you remember is gone. The cancer's done ate up his body. You need to be ready before you go in there."

9

When I was a child, the rear parlor was the farm office. After supper, Dad would close the door, settle behind the desk, and figure out which bills could be paid and which would have to be delayed. Even in the best years, decisions had to be made. In the more-common lean years, though, a foul mood emanated from this room. Dean and I avoided entering, knowing we risked being enveloped by the darkness.

This was also the room where punishments were meted out —a judge's chamber. If we brought a note home from school or a neighbor called about some misdeed, we would be summoned and have to stand in front of that desk for the inquisition.

Arguing was futile. We were usually guilty of the crime, of course, but even the rare times we weren't, the word of an adult always outweighed ours.

Dean accepted that as a simple fact of life. He didn't really fear punishment anyway. Besides, he reasoned he got away with mischief sometimes, so it all balanced out.

I struggled with the unfairness. I cowered everywhere else in life but always pushed back at home. I knew my defiance invited harsher repercussions, but that made me even more argumentative the next time. As a result, it felt like I spent half my teenaged years grounded with a host of extra chores.

Mom said Dad had grown too weak to climb the stairs to the second-floor bedroom they shared, so they had shoved the desk in the parlor against the wall and brought in a hospital bed. Hospice came by to check on him and ensure he had everything he needed to be comfortable. The only alternative was to lie in some generic hospital bed, surrounded by noise and strangers. They didn't need the office since they were no longer running a farm, so it made sense to convert it to a hospital room.

I steadied myself against the doorframe, my legs too weak from the shock of seeing him to hold me without the extra support. Mom stood beside me, her arm around my waist and head resting against my shoulder.

The room smelled warm and moist, a hint of rot and decay despite the fresh air drifting through the open window. The lights were turned off—too bright for Dad's eyes, she explained —but sunlight filtered through the sheers flapping in the breeze.

The spreading cancer had consumed his bulk. The husk rattling on the bed seemed inconsequential, a mere whisper of what he'd once been. His bony arms rested on the top of a blanket that hid the shadow of his body underneath, little more than a ripple in the linens. The only movement was a shaky rising and falling of his chest. His mouth hung open between gaunt cheeks. The cloudy eyes stared from sunken sockets and struggled to focus.

I hesitated to make any noise. I debated leaving—even inched back from the door—but Mom's presence held me in place.

Just as I wondered if he was even conscious, Dad's tongue flicked out of his mouth and ran across his cracked lips. I forced myself forward on unsteady feet, leaving Mom watching me from the doorway. My fingers tingled, and my stomach tumbled, threatening to disgorge the sandwich I'd just eaten. About halfway across the room, I halted and whispered, "Dad?"

A sound choked out from the body in front of me, an attempt at speech. A clicking noise echoed as he swallowed to clear his throat. He uttered a second effort. The word was a wisp of wind, but it hit with the brutality of a tornado. "Dean?"

The sting of the question hammered me. Years of resenting being compared to my brother bubbled up, but now was not the time. I fought to remember Mom's caution about his mental fogginess. I swallowed the anger that threatened to erupt inside me. "It's Mav…"

He wouldn't know me as Mad Maverick. I had never been that in this house. When I'd tried earlier to tell Mom that I was now known by the nickname, she simply replied, "Not by me." That had ended the discussion, so I corrected myself here. "It's Freddie."

His head turned toward me. His eyes squinted but seemed to focus somewhere behind me. "Freddie?"

Was it recognition? Or was he just repeating what I'd said? I hated the tremble in my voice as I struggled to answer. "Yes, sir."

He tried to push his arms under his body to raise himself up from the bed, but he moved only a few inches before collapsing into the pillows. He raised a quivering hand and beckoned with a thin finger. "Come closer. My eyes are…" He swallowed. "Everything's a fog."

Sweat rolled down my back. I took a hesitant step forward like a disobedient child being beckoned by his father. The finger continued to urge me closer until I brushed up against the cold metal of the safety rails on the bed. Dry fingers wrapped around my wrist. Death rattled in those digits. Dad's eyes blinked as he struggled to speak, each word breathless and slow. "It's you."

The saliva in my mouth dried up. My voice came out raspy. "Yes, Dad."

"I'm glad you came before…"

For the second time that day, tears welled up. I hadn't wanted to return to this place. I'd done it only out of duty. I didn't expect to feel anything else. But now, standing here with the dying man's grip on me, grief and sorrow flooded through my body and confused me with their presence. "How are you…" The question seemed wrong considering the man's appearance, but I could think of nothing else. "Feeling?"

A bark escaped Skeeter. Maybe it was laughter, though I couldn't be sure. He pointed with a shaky finger at the dangling IV bag. "When it gets to be too much, I press a little button and start floating. Doesn't make all the pain go away, but makes me not care. Sounds awful, but at this point, not caring ain't so bad."

I followed the tubing from the back of his hand. "Morphine?"

Dad's finger touched the tip of his nose. "Bingo. Ain't no worries about getting addicted now." His eyes fluttered closed. "But it makes me so drowsy."

Growing up, he'd lectured us on the vices lurking to distract boys from a good life. Alcohol. Tobacco. Sex. Drugs. Especially drugs. Legal and illegal. He didn't like taking an aspirin, so I struggled to understand how much pain he must have been in to agree to liquid relief dripped into his veins. "Does it help?"

His scrawny shoulders rose in the slightest of shrugs. A clicking came from his throat as his Adam's apple bobbed. A cough slipped out, and he pointed with a shaky finger at a glass on a table. A straw protruded at an angle.

I turned to see if Mom was coming to help, but she had

slipped away, leaving me alone with him. He coughed again, so I picked up the glass to hand it to him, but he didn't take it. His chapped lips parted, and I slid the straw between them. He sipped, swallowed, then sipped again before falling back into the pillow with a mutter of thanks.

After settling the glass back onto the table, I watched him, shifting my feet and unsure what to say. "Are you hungry? I can get Mom to bring a sandwich. Or soup."

He shook his head. "Nothing stays down."

"Oh." I looked through the empty doorway, silently begging Mom to return. When she didn't, I looked through the slats of the blinds. "Crops look good. Harvest should be strong." I regretted the words as soon as they slipped out of my mouth, but I couldn't think of what else to say.

He smacked his lips. "Good for Russ." His eyelids drifted closed.

I took a step back from the bed. "You want me to let you take a nap?"

He forced his eyes open, but they slowly slid shut again. He mumbled, "Just sit with me for a bit."

The chair sat near the head of his bed. A book Mom was reading waited on the arm, a slip of paper marking her spot. A cardigan draped over the back would ward off any chills she felt. That was her place to be, not mine. "I can come back later."

"Not much later left. I gotta…" His voice faded and was replaced with a soft breathing.

Trembling, I backed toward the door, my eyes locked on the sleeping form. My butt brushed against the dresser, startling me. I turned and ran down the hallway.

Mom stepped out of the kitchen, wiping her hands on her apron. Worry etched her face. "Are you okay?"

I tried to answer, but nothing came out. My pulse raced. I

gasped for air, memories of childhood asthma attacks haunting me, though I'd long since stopped using an inhaler.

Unable to stay in the house for another minute, I raced out the screen door and to my car. As I tore down the driveway, I could see her standing on the porch, wringing her hands in worry.

She would just have to deal with it. I would explain when I came back.

In the back of my mind, a voice whispered, *If I come back.*

10

The curves in the road were too sharp. I was going way too fast. I did too much city driving and not enough country roads now. The tears clogging my eyes weren't helping. Instead of slowing down, though, I pushed my foot harder against the accelerator, weighted down by waves of grief.

With each snaking turn, the tires squealed. The colossal beast of a machine swayed and pulled me farther and farther across the yellow line with each twist. I fought the steering wheel harder and harder to maintain control.

Then came the curve that was too much to handle. The SUV slid sideways, and I overcorrected. The Escalade fishtailed. Its weight sent it into an uncontrollable spin. In the commotion of screeching tires and smoke from burning rubber, the rear became the front. I hurtled backward down the road, unable to clearly see where I was heading. I slammed on the brakes.

Was this the panic Dean experienced in the last seconds of his life? Had he known he was going to crash? Did he feel the tentacles of death wrap around his heart before he hit that tree? Or had he been as confident as ever, convinced he would save himself once again? Maybe he'd believed he would walk away with only a few scratches and bruises, less banged up than after a good football game. Maybe he'd truly believed he would avoid a collision entirely.

I had no such illusion. A grove of trees grew in my rearview mirror. The steering wheel wobbled in my hands, a useless rudder in an out-of-control skid.

Then the rear tire dropped off the edge of the pavement and sank into the soft dirt. My top-heavy vehicle shuddered when the momentum slowed. The driver's side rose. The vehicle threatened to roll.

A low-hanging branch slapped the back window, as loud as a cannon retort in the confines of the cabin. A crack slithered across the glass. My body tensed in anticipation of a greater impact. I closed my eyes and prayed.

Then it was quiet. The vehicle had, somehow, come to a stop with two tires still on the road. I leaned my head against the steering wheel and closed my eyes. My body quaked with fear and relief. A thin sheen of sweat formed over my body. I took a deep breath to calm my nerves. A wail escaped my lips.

Seeing my father—a stern, healthy man in my mind—as little more than a withering body in a deathbed was too much. I'd wanted only to escape the pain and anguish so badly that I had driven faster than I had in years. Much too fast for these country roads, especially in this ridiculously big SUV.

On unsteady feet, I walked around the vehicle, inspecting for damage. Scratches from tree limbs etched the paint. A tail-light was shattered. The rear window sported a thick crack. But somehow, I had avoided plunging off the road and into the forest, where I would have ended up wrapped around a tree. Just like Dean had.

I lowered my head against the side of the car and sobbed. My emotions confounded me. Just a day earlier, I'd told myself I'd felt so indifferent that I hadn't even wanted to return to

Millerton. But if that were true, why was the sense of immi-
nent loss so great? How could I lose something when I hadn't
even seen the man for nearly two decades?

The obvious answer shook me—because I cared more than
I had ever admitted to myself.

My breathing slowed as I contemplated that thought. The
tears dwindled. I took a shaky breath.

Opening my eyes, I focused on the deep skid marks painted
across the asphalt. Fortunately, no oncoming traffic had been
on the blind sides of the curves. Not a single vehicle
approached as I sat on the side of the road. Chalk one up in
favor of the isolation of Miller County. I needed to extract my
car before that changed.

The tires on the passenger side were sunk about three
inches into the soft shoulder. Not hard to escape. I'd pulled
myself out of far worse messes as a teen in a significantly less
capable car. The four-wheel drive would have me back on the
road in minutes.

But where would I go? Back to the house. Eventually. That
much I had decided. Whatever doubts I had harbored
moments earlier were squashed, even if I dreaded the coming
days.

But returning to the house without time to think wasn't
possible. I needed to compose myself and wrestle with my feelings. I needed a quiet spot to meditate.

Getting back on the road and turned around only took a
couple minutes, but this time, I kept my speed well below the
limit. My luck had been pushed as far as I dared.

As I neared the edge of town, the number of houses grew.
A few businesses dotted the road. Then the town's park, a place
of so many childhood memories, came into view. Maybe my
subconscious had known all along where I needed to go and
guided me in this direction. The park had the perfect spot to
get away from everything.

Not the sports fields near the main parking lot, where crowds gathered, watching kids' games—baseball on one end and soccer on the other. I had spent hours in those bleachers, watching my brother's rise to fame. By the time we'd entered middle school, everyone knew he would make any of the teams he wanted.

The hiking trails that circled through the woods didn't offer the sanctuary I sought either. On a pretty day in June, families with squawking little kids would traverse the paths, stopping at informational signs and learning about nature. Too much noise and too many people to think.

But there was a remote corner of the park, where few people visited. A narrow, winding trail led deep into the forest until it opened into a small meadow. Wildflowers exploded with color as bees buzzed through the air. No picnic tables or benches enticed casual visitors, despite the surrounding beauty. Only the hardy went to that spot, so it was a perfect place to be alone.

During my teen years, I had spent many hours in that hidden meadow, scribbling in a journal, making up songs, and daydreaming of playing them in front of screaming fans. Sometimes, I sat there alone with a guitar in my hands, strumming chords and picking through notes. Other days, Xander drummed rhythms on the barks of trees. Either was far better than being forced to watch Dean score yet another goal and lead his team to yet another victory. It was our sanctuary.

The trail remained etched in my mind, and I followed the path without hesitation. At the first turn, the parking lot disappeared behind a thick layer of leaves. The sounds of cars and cheering fans dwindled. Squirrels scampered about, their claws scrabbling across bark. An unseen hawk shrieked as it stalked a meal. Tree branches clacked in the gentle breeze.

The deeper into the forest I walked, the calmer I became.

The tension seeped out of my tight muscles. My chest loosened. My freed mind grappled with the conflicts in my head.

In this more emotionally controlled state, I could envision the impact of my father dying without panicking. How would my aging mother, always so resilient in my memories, handle living alone? Would Russ honor his commitment to let her live out her years in that house?

My thoughts were distracted by an unexpected sound. From a distance, the chords of an acoustic guitar floated in the air. The song was unfamiliar. Slow. Melodic. Beautiful.

Someone had beaten me to my oasis. I would have to find somewhere else, but I didn't resent the intrusion. The music was too interesting. Who played so beautifully? Who had written the haunting melody? My listening tastes were eclectic and wide-ranging. I knew many obscure artists, but I couldn't place this one. Intrigued, I pushed forward, tiptoeing down the trail. I didn't want to disturb whoever was there, but I wanted to be close enough to hear the song more clearly.

The trees thinned. Sunlight filtered through the branches. The meadow came into view. Sitting with his back against a broad oak, eyes closed, a teenaged boy strummed a guitar. He sang softly, lyrics I couldn't place. I inched toward the opening of the trail, mesmerized.

Despite my effort at stealth, my foot came down on a twig, snapping it in half. In the meadow's quiet, it sounded like a crack of a rifle, loud and rude. The boy's eyes popped open. His hand froze over the strings. The music stopped. He searched the perimeter. It didn't take long before he focused on me.

I had intruded on his solitude. How many times had I wanted the same solitude as a teen, just to be alone with my songs, only to have some clueless adult interfere? I did my best to apologize. "Sorry for interrupting."

The boy didn't respond. He only stared at me. The

awkwardness made me feel compelled to explain. "The song. I had never heard it. It's really… good."

He looked down at the guitar in his hand and shrugged. "It's not finished. I'm still working on it."

An open notebook lay to his side, a pen keeping the pages from flapping in the breeze.

I was incredulous. "You wrote it?"

When the boy only nodded, I tried to explain my interest. "I'm a musician. Written a few songs myself."

"I know who you are. You're Mad Maverick McDougal."

My mouth dropped open in shock at being recognized.

11

G rowing up, I'd dreamed of escaping Millerton to go be a rock star. Playing in front of screaming fans in sold-out arenas. Traveling in chauffeured limousines. Staying in high-end hotels. Signing autographs by the dozens. Walking down the street being hounded by paparazzi. And, yeah, women throwing themselves at me.

None of it had come true. Truthfully, I was a big unknown.

I had been a part of so many bands since leaving Millerton that I couldn't name them all. We booked whatever gigs we could find, mostly bars, festivals, and fraternity houses. We rode to shows in vans overflowing with our equipment and served as our own roadies. The best we could afford were cheap rooms in fleabag motels, and we had to share even those. I had spent more than a few nights sleeping in a car in the parking lot of some nightclub.

Those jobs lasted a few days or weeks, then I was on to the next group. When I couldn't hook up with a band, I played in restaurants or on street corners for tips. To supplement that, I bussed tables, washed dishes, and mopped floors. Whatever it took. Rarely did anyone recognize me or ask for my autograph.

A few years back, I'd had a brief taste of fame. A friend who played bass got me a gig playing lead guitar for Exploding Oatmeal. Stupid name, but I had heard worse.

The lead singer was a young guy with an okay voice, which we could make passable with electronics. The songs he wrote were bubblegum crap. The same guitar chords played over and over. A bass line that never changed. An unimaginative drum rhythm.

He made up for his lack of talent with his looks. His ever-present smile revealed a row of glistening white teeth, perfectly aligned thanks to his divorced parents who catered to his every whim in some weird competition to prove who loved him more.

His always-open shirt exposed a smooth chest. A gym membership guaranteed a lean muscularity. Tight skinny jeans highlighted his bulge. We weren't supposed to discuss the fact that it was amplified with a strategically placed sock.

Somehow, he mixed that sex appeal with an awe-shucks demeanor that made him seem approachable and sweet. The girls—most were too young to drive themselves to our shows—went crazy for him. Their parents fell for his clean-cut image. On stage, he appeared to be the nicest guy they'd ever met. Just a sweet, innocent kid so blessed to have this opportunity.

Behind the scenes, though, he was a total jerk. He fired me—and everyone else in the band—at least once a week, usually in a kicking, screaming temper tantrum that rivaled a tired toddler's. He claimed none of us had any talent and were holding him back. We should be grateful he tolerated us.

But then things would blow over, and we moved on to the next gig. The truth was that any of us were better than him. Together, we kept the music going as he pranced around the stage to the shrieks of his adoring fans.

As much as we all hated him, the work was steady and the money solid. I'd been part of more talented bands who played more original songs, but this was the first that brought a real promise of financial stability. I was tired of being behind on rent and eating ramen noodles, so I put up with it.

We'd become a YouTube and TikTok darling. At least, he had. We were decidedly in the background as he danced around, shaking his skinny ass with his shirt open to his navel. We were just props for him to use, but props with a paycheck.

We toured some small stages but sold them out thanks to those screaming girls and their indulgent parents. Crying teens begged for tickets on video.

Suddenly, we were hot. A manager came on board with grandiose plans to make us superstars. We scored some real time in a real recording studio and cut a debut album. Its release met critical condemnation but respectable sales. A concert tour was planned for big stages and even some arenas. International dates were scheduled. We were rocketing to stardom. Nothing could stop us.

Except a damned virus.

Covid hit, and lockdowns shut down performances. Our tour was postponed then canceled. The big budgets dried up, and our money stopped flowing. We went our separate ways, holed up in our apartments—him in his mother's big house—and waited for rehearsals to restart.

While we twiddled our thumbs, the screaming girls grew a year older. Their interests moved on. Our video views dwindled. Album sales tanked. In a fit of rage, the lead singer fired us all. He hired new musicians and kept the band's name.

I found out in a video, of course. He appeared shirtless one evening on a viral post. One glance told me he'd spent his lockdown working out in the home gym his mother had set up for him in her basement. The camera was strategically positioned to show his unmade bed behind, a not-so-subtle hint to those girls to come flocking back to him.

It worked. He hit it big.

Exploding Oatmeal sold out arenas and cut a second album to even more critical scorn but huge commercial success. No one cared that the musicians behind the lead singer had changed. He'd kept the same boring chords, bass lines, and percussion rhythms.

Their stupid songs played everywhere. I couldn't escape them. In the ultimate irony, I was playing guitar in a restaurant one night and taking requests. Someone asked for an Exploding Oatmeal song. They didn't recognize my connection. They didn't recognize me. I had no fame. No fortune.

So how did this kid know who I was? He didn't strike me as an Exploding Oatmeal fan. He was certainly too young to get into the bars my other bands had played. His answer didn't clarify my confusion. "You're from Millerton."

"Do you know everyone who grew up here?"

"No, but I know everyone from here who made a living playing guitar. That's basically you."

Good point, though I wasn't sure scraping by the way I had qualified as a living.

"I have posters in my room of awesome guitar players." The kid counted off the names on his fingers. "Carlos Santana. B.B. King. Eric Clapton. Jimi Hendrix. Steve Vai. Mark Tremonti. Jonny Lang. James McVey. John Mayer."

I interrupted him. "You have a poster of me?"

"Didn't know there was one of you." He snickered, set the guitar down on the grass beside him, and leaned back against the tree. "I've seen some of your stuff on YouTube, though. Exploding Oatmeal is pretty good."

"But—"

"I know. Artistic differences. Went in a different direction. All the usual crap they say when they fire someone."

"Yeah, well—"

"The band they put together for the second album is pretty good."

"That hurts."

"It shouldn't. How many people know the name of the guitarist of One Direction?"

"Dan Richards," I answered.

He nodded his approval, but I knew what he meant. Most people thought of one of the world's most famous musical acts as five guys. They didn't even think about the musicians in the shadows of the stage. "Is that what you want to be? A rock-and-roll guitarist?"

"Sometimes. Maybe not rock. Caleb Smith of Balsam Range is awesome. And he doesn't just play. He makes guitars." He pursed his lips in thought. "Or maybe I write music."

"That song you were just playing. It was amazing."

His face reddened. "Thanks. It's not ready yet for people to hear it."

I looked around the clearing, remembering my own days of hanging out here alone with my thoughts. "That's why you come here? To write?"

"Yeah. When I can get my parents to bring me." He looked up. "I got my license back in March but don't have a car. I borrow Mom's when I can, but…"

I nodded, remembering how hard I'd saved my busking money to buy my own car.

His face scrunched into a question. "Why call yourself Mad Maverick? Because of that bar fight in Alabama? You really take a gun away from some guy?"

His change in direction threw me off guard. The story had been told and retold so many times that it had taken on legendary status. Like most legends, there was a kernel of truth to it but not much more than that. I would not tell what really happened to some kid who would post it on social media, though. "It was a long time ago."

"Why not just call yourself Freddie?"

I shrugged. "Mad Maverick is a better stage name than Freddie."

"Freddie Mercury would disagree."

The kid knew how to get under my skin. Or maybe he just didn't have much of a filter. Couldn't say I had one when I was his age either. At sixteen, I was a master at being abrasive. What he said next, though, made me forget any annoyance.

"I like your solo stuff better."

Puzzled, I answered, "I've never recorded anything solo."

He smiled and picked up his guitar. His long fingers wrapped around the neck and expertly pinned the strings to the frets as he strummed. His voice was soulful, melding beautifully with the chords as he played a song I hadn't done for years. He played it slower than I did and sang higher notes than I'd ever attempted. The song, one of my favorites, was beautiful in his performance, better than I had ever done it. When he was finished, I asked where he'd heard it.

"Saw it on YouTube. Somebody recorded you playing it in a restaurant."

I didn't know that and made a mental note to look it up. Since it was performed in a public place, though, he hadn't heard the full song, the one I played only to myself. "My favorite part is a riff I added after the second stanza, but I couldn't play it in restaurants. Managers want the songs all to be quiet and not disturb the diners in the main dining room. Or, if you're playing in the bar, really loud to encourage booze sales. Nothing in between and nothing to draw too much attention away from what they're pushing."

He held out his guitar. "Show me."

I hesitated. What I had said wasn't entirely true. Some restaurant managers wanted the music as background noise, but others would have been fine with me playing the songs however I wanted. The truth was that some music was for public consumption. Other music was meant to be private. I had never shared the riff.

But this kid's face was so open and eager to listen. His eyes glistened with interest. And I was still buzzing from hearing him playing one of my songs so well.

Taking his offered guitar, I sat down on the grass and ran through the song again. When I came to the riff, I closed my eyes and let the notes flow from my mind through my arms and out of my tingling fingers. When I finished, he asked me to play it again. He joined me, singing in harmony as if we'd practiced for days.

When I finished the second time, he took back the guitar and leaned against the tree. He played the notes I had just performed, slowly and carefully but almost perfectly. At one point, he paused with his fingers hovering over the strings and asked me to explain a part he had missed. When I answered, he smiled, nodded, then played it back to me, hitting all the notes.

Satisfied, he went back to the beginning of the song and began to play. We sang it in a duet, him taking the higher notes as I dropped down in harmony. When we hit the added section, I watched as his fingers flew over the strings. He played back what I'd done, adding his own touches to what I'd shown him. He was better at sixteen than I had been at his age.

Honestly, he was a better guitar player at sixteen than I'd ever been. Not only fast but also soulful. He didn't just play the music. He lived it. It flowed through him.

When we finished, he rested the instrument in his lap and looked directly at me. "You're home for your dad, right?"

I nodded.

"Do you have a guitar here?"

I thought of the one I had picked up at Xander's store. "Actually, yes."

"Bring it tomorrow. I'll get my mom's car and meet you here. If you want. Would be fun."

Before I could agree, a voice from the woods behind me interrupted us. "Harrison?"

The boy glanced at the clock on his phone and rolled his eyes. He let out a sigh of exasperation and called out, "Down here, Dad."

"Figured as much. You're supposed to be up at the fields, watching your brother's baseball game. Didn't we tell you not to run off?" I turned just in time to see Russ Caldwell step into the clearing. He froze midstride, his eyes locked on me and his mouth hung open in shock.

12

S everal seconds ticked by as Russ stood at the entrance to
the clearing. His eyes bounced from me to Harrison and
back as his mouth opened and closed while he was apparently
debating what he wanted to say. When he finally spoke, he kept
his tone calm, though I could hear the tension in his voice.
"Been a long time, Freddie."

As I struggled to think of a response, he turned his attention to the teenager beside me. "What are you two talking
about?"

Harrison stood and brushed the grass off his jeans. He held
up the guitar with a grip around its neck and answered,
"Music."

Russ's eyes darted toward me. "Just music?"

"Yes, Dad, that's all." Harrison emphasized the *dad* in that
way teens had of expressing sarcasm while being able to maintain plausible deniability. I knew it well because of how
frequently I had used it.

Before I could join in the awkward conversation, Sarah
Franklin—though I guessed it was Sarah Caldwell now—
appeared on the path behind Russ. She held hands with a boy

and girl, both about ten years old. The boy wore a Little League baseball uniform, and the girl was in a soccer jersey. Sarah pulled up short beside Russ and eyed me sternly. She looked no happier to see me than did Russ. Her voice was icy when she spoke. "Hello, Freddie."

I stammered a hello back.

"These are our children, Brandon and Brenda. I see you've already met Harrison."

When I'd first stumbled upon Harrison, I hadn't thought about the familiarity of his looks. Now that I was seeing him and Sarah together, I could see the resemblance. The eyes. The shape of the nose. His jaw was sharper, and he was taller, but the connection was obvious. "He's very talented. I'm sure he gets that from you."

I had meant it as a compliment, but I didn't think of how Russ might hear it as a dig until Sarah glanced at her husband. He hadn't reacted at all. Softly, she agreed, "I suppose."

Harrison said, "He's going to bring his guitar tomorrow. We're going to play together." He hesitated. "If I can borrow the car."

Sarah and Russ exchanged a glance before she answered, "You could do that at the house."

"Please," he begged. "It's more private here."

I knew what he meant. I'd never enjoyed practicing within earshot of Dean for fear he would tease me about something. It was probably the same with his younger siblings.

Besides, no way would I feel comfortable in Russ's presence. Playing guitar or not. I wasn't even sure I wanted to meet Harrison again anywhere now that I knew whose kid he was.

Sarah saved me from answering. She let go of her kids' hands and gently touched Russ's arm. He nodded slightly to her and addressed Harrison. "Get your guitar, and let's go. We'll talk when we get home."

Harrison shot me a look and nodded. He scooped up his

notebook and marched up the trail with his brother and sister in tow.

When they disappeared around the bend, Russ hesitated before speaking. "I'm sorry about Skeeter. He's a good man."

Playing music had given me an escape from my emotions, but the reminder of my father brought it back. My eyes teared up, and I looked away.

He put his arm around Sarah and turned toward the path, but she motioned for him to go on. He hesitated, glanced over at me, then nodded.

Once he disappeared into the woods, Sarah took a few steps toward me. "Libby told us you were coming. You seen your dad yet?"

I nodded. "Just a bit ago. Came here to clear my head."

"You always did like this spot."

A butterfly drifted lazily across the meadow and settled on a blooming wildflower. The air smelled fresher and cleaner than I remembered. Only if I strained could I hear the sounds of voices from the ballfields in the main park. "Must be a musician thing. Harrison seems to have found it too."

"I showed him a couple years ago. He was so shy about the guitar in front of others, but down here, he could let loose. Ever since he got his driver's license this spring, this has been his favorite place to come." She smiled for the first time since coming down the path. I'd forgotten how much that smile used to light up my days.

"He shouldn't be shy as talented as he is."

"You of all people should know how hard it is as a teen. I used to have to beg you to play in front of friends."

We stood awkwardly, not remembering how to talk to each other.

"I didn't know he was your kid when I said we'd play guitar together. I can make up an excuse not to if that's easier."

She hesitated.

I held my breath, half-afraid she would accept my offer and half-worried she would refuse it.

Finally, she said, "I think it might be good for him. For both of you."

"If you're sure."

"Not too many people at his talent level around here. I know you know what that's like."

The bitterness in her words stung. I'd said that same thing so many times in high school without ever thinking of how she and Xander might take those thoughts. The implication that I'd included them in that assessment was clear. I couldn't even deny the truth in it. And I hadn't given them the simple courtesy of a goodbye, much less an explanation. "I'm sorry I left the way I did. I should have handled it better."

"Yeah, you should have."

I didn't have a response to that. She turned away from me and looked up the trail where her family had disappeared. As much to herself as to me, she said, "I need to catch up with Russ."

I blurted out what I had been thinking. "You two together surprises me."

Her head snapped back at me, and fierceness filled her eyes. "Why? His best friend died in a wreck. My best friend disappeared without saying goodbye. We were both grieving, trying to fill these sudden voids in our lives. Without anyone to turn to, we leaned on each other. Talked. Listened. Cried. And fell in love."

"But you barely spoke to him in high school. We ran with a different crowd."

"You ran with a different crowd. Always you against the villains." She shook her head slowly and took a deep breath. She continued, quieter. "We went to a small school. Why wouldn't I talk to everybody? Russ. Blake. Dean."

"I know you talked to Dean. I caught you."

"Caught? That's exactly what I mean. We weren't hiding anything."

"He asked you out, didn't he?"

"Yeah, he did. And I said no. When he asked why, I told him because we were dating. He was shocked." She pointed a finger at me. "You were the one hiding. You never told your own brother about us. Were you ashamed of it?"

"No, of course not."

"That's what was going on when you came out to that parking lot and 'caught' us." She made air quotes with her hands. "We were having an honest conversation like friends do."

She turned toward the trail and walked away from me. When she reached the edge of the clearing, she paused and turned back to me. "I'll make a deal."

I waited. What else could I do?

"I'll let Harrison come here and play guitar with you. In return, you make me a promise."

"What?"

"When you leave—whether it's tomorrow or the next day or next week—you say goodbye to Harrison. Don't you dare leave him hanging the way you did me."

I nodded.

"That's not enough. I want to hear it. I will not allow you to hurt Harrison. Promise."

"I promise. And thanks for doing that for me."

"I'm not doing it for you. I'm doing it for Harrison."

With that, she turned and disappeared up the trail.

13

S hiny new homes dotted the surrounding mountains. They were built for retirees or as summer houses for people escaping the heat of Florida or the crowds of New York, Atlanta, or Charlotte. In the dead of winter, those mountains were dark. In the summer, the lights from the homes flickered from the slopes like distant fireflies flittering far above us.

When the houses' occupants came down into the valleys, they headed to Asheville, Hendersonville, or Waynesville—places with restaurants, shopping, and art galleries.

They didn't come to Millerton. No one did. It was a place people were from, not a destination.

Sarah was the exception. Her father had grown up in Millerton and left for college, a common path. He'd married and lived in Charlotte with his wife and daughter, Sarah. When they divorced, he'd moved back to Millerton, sold insurance from a storefront, married a local woman, and moved into the house between Xander and Blake. Sarah had stayed with her mother, except for a few weeks each summer with her father.

Her annual arrival caused a stir. She was an outsider, of course, someone we didn't see every day at school. She carried a spice of big-city sophistication we weren't accustomed to. But unlike a lot of the visitors who flocked to the mountains, she didn't think of herself as above us. She was friendly to everyone and fun to hang around.

As if that weren't enough, she was beautiful. Each summer, she grew prettier. Bright, sparkling eyes. Thick, luscious hair. Ever-developing curves to her body. I suspected every boy in Millerton fantasized about her. During her summer weeks in Millerton, she had a constant stream of boys hanging out on her porch, under the watchful eye of her father.

Xander also monitored the comings and goings. The day she arrived each summer, he would call me and announce the news. From his den, he could peer through his blinds and watch her without her knowledge. He would bitterly tell me about boys who chatted for hours with her, asked her out on dates, or attempted to kiss her. And he gleefully shared the times he saw her reject a suitor.

Blake certainly noticed her, too, though he was less circumspect. He was often sitting on her front steps, much to Xander's disgust. That, of course, meant his best friends Dean and Russ were there, along with most of the other popular kids from school. We waited for them to leave before visiting her.

Someone like Sarah would normally never give losers like Xander and me the time of day, but she was different. She was as friendly to us as she was to them. Maybe she didn't stay in Millerton long enough each year to learn the social pecking order. Or maybe she just didn't care about cliques.

Our attraction to her only grew when we discovered she loved to sing. When she found out I played, she asked me to bring my guitar to her porch. I learned dozens of songs just because she wanted to sing them and I didn't want to disappoint her.

The first time I played in front of a group of people was on her porch. We were thirteen. My hormones were running rampant. A sudden squeak in my voice would punctuate every other sentence. A whiff of her shampoo drove me wild, the memory of which would feed many a late-night fantasy when I was alone in my dark room.

When Blake and a mob of his buddies interrupted one of our music sessions on her porch, I wanted to slip away, but she stopped me. She begged me to accompany her in a song. Nervously, I picked my way through the first chords. When her voice rose into the air, the thought of our audience disappeared, and the notes came flawlessly to me. My fingers danced, building the foundation for her voice as it soared.

When the song ended, the other boys cheered. She beamed, wrapped her arms around me, and hugged.

Blake shouted, "More! More!"

I didn't have a choice but to continue. Partially because I couldn't move the guitar out of my lap without displaying how her hug had affected me. More because I didn't want to disappoint her. Mostly, though, their applause tickled my soul.

Of course, they were celebrating her voice more than my guitar, but I was there. I was a part of the song. I wasn't the shy kid sitting in the back corner away from the action. My peers, who only had ever seemed to know me as Dean's brother, were applauding me. It was my first taste of what it was like to play music for others, even if they were just other kids from school.

THE HEAT CAME EARLY in the middle of May, several weeks before the start of the summer vacation between our junior and senior years. We saw it as the last summer of childhood freedom. A year later, some would be preparing for college. Others would be taking jobs in the local mills or on the farms. A few would head off to the military. I was already mapping out a plan to pursue my rock-and-roll dream.

Early one Saturday morning, Xander called me at the house with exciting news. Sarah had arrived early. She almost never came for a weekend, so we didn't know what it meant.

I hurriedly finished my chores and took off for town in the clunker of a car I'd bought with my busking money. She wasn't on her porch when I arrived, so I walked into Xander's house without knocking on the door. Anna would already be down at the store, so I never knocked.

Xander was standing in the den at the side window, peering through the blinds, hoping to catch a glimpse of Sarah. His infatuation with her had grown over the years. His fantasy had evolved to the two of them marrying, moving to Charlotte, and raising perfect children. He didn't have a job in this narrative, but it didn't really matter. It was just another childhood dream that would never come true.

We paced, chatted nervously, and paced some more. Every few minutes, he would walk over to the blinds and peer through. His fear, uttered over and over, was that Blake would see her outside and get to her first.

When he parted the blinds and gasped, I knew she was there. I raced over and looked out the window. She sat on their porch swing, rocking slowly. Alone. No Blake in sight.

Xander beat me out the front door because I paused to grab my guitar, but I was right on his heels. We were climbing the short flight of steps to her porch when we saw the tears in her eyes. When we asked why, she blurted, "My mom died."

My heart cratered. Our excitement at seeing her turned to a crushing sorrow. Our ill-conceived fantasies of asking her out vanished. Our friend was hurting and needed us.

I sat on one side of her on that porch swing and Xander on the other, rocking and talking throughout the day. We let her tell the story haltingly as she struggled to explain.

Her mother had dropped her off at school, waved goodbye, and headed to her office job downtown. A speeding driver had cut her mother's car off on the interstate, clipping the front bumper and sending it careening into the concrete barrier. The car had come to rest in front of a semi with brakes squealing as it tried—and failed—to stop in time. Firefighters struggled to cut her out of the car. Paramedics rushed her to the hospital. The principal knocked on the classroom door and asked for Sarah. Then came the horrifying news and the suddenness of being alone. Her father arrived a few hours later and held her as she sobbed.

We didn't ask questions. We didn't really need any more details. All we could do was sit with her and listen. Sometimes, she spoke clearly. Sometimes, the words devolved into sobs.

Blake came over midmorning, heard the news, and hugged her. Rough, tough Blake reduced to teary eyes. Soon after he left, word spread quickly. In small towns, it never took long. Others came and went throughout the day, but we didn't leave her side until it was fully dark and she finally went inside.

We arrived early again on Sunday and sat with her. Monday, we had school but joined her as soon as classes were over. We let her talk about her mom, her life in Charlotte, and her friends back there. The teachers at her old school said she'd done enough work to pass her courses for the junior year. She was moving to Millerton for her senior year, was going to graduate with us then return to the city and her old life.

On the fourth day, we arrived after school to see her rocking in the swing. When we mounted the steps, she stood and shook her head. "Let's go do something. I'm tired of sitting here."

I looked at my old Honda Civic sitting in Xander's drive. Neither one of them owned a car, so that put the onus on me. And I was never sure if the old thing was going to break down. "Where?"

She closed her eyes and thought. "I've never seen where you rehearse."

Xander shrugged. "It's just the back of my mom's store."

"Sounds cool. Let's go."

She stuck her head in the door and told her father. After the usual admonishments from him—"Drive safe, and be home before supper"—we piled into my car and headed the few blocks to downtown. With a wave to Xander's mom as we passed through the store, we carried my guitar and amp into the converted space in the rear. Xander's drums waited in the corner.

"Play something," she begged, so we did. Slow and mournful to match our spirits. I sang the opening chorus with my weak, warbling voice. When she joined in, I let her take the lead. Her voice rose, echoing off the brick walls.

When the song ended, we stood looking at each other. A slow clap drew our attention to the rear entrance to the store. Anna Stewart leaned against the doorframe and applauded.

The Wicked Centipedes were born.

14

_____

Dejected and tired, I swung by the consignment store to talk to the only friendly face I knew, but the lights were out. The doors were locked. Xander didn't answer my repeated rapping on the glass.

I put my ear against the glass and listened for the sound of his drumming. He'd said he'd quit playing, though I couldn't grasp how anyone could walk away from music. Maybe stopping by earlier, spending some time playing with him, had rekindled that spark in him.

But I heard nothing, so I could only guess he had left. I looked around for his car only to realize I didn't know what he drove. He didn't have one when we were teens. He'd borrowed Anna's until I'd scraped together the cash for my own.

Standing on that empty sidewalk with my hands in my pockets, I debated how to find him. He hadn't said where he lived now. Did he still have his old family home? Did he keep it after she died? Or did he sell it?

Driving by didn't answer the question. The lights were off. No car sat in his driveway. Did that mean he was out with friends, getting a bite to eat or a cold drink? Which friends? We hadn't talked about who he hung out with now.

I pulled my cell phone out of my pocket and stared at it. Neither of us had one in high school. Few kids did in those days. I doubted it would have worked out at the farm back then, and Xander never had any money. But surely, he had one now. Everyone did. But I hadn't thought to ask for his number, so I couldn't call.

Loneliness gripped me. Growing up, I'd embraced my loner status. Reveled in it. Worn it like a badge of honor. I was so cool I didn't need to hang with the popular kids. I'd lived it so much, I almost believed it.

But was it them? Or was it me? After all, adulthood hadn't changed my cavalier attitude. My contacts in my phone were old bandmates, club owners, or other music connections. *Are any of them really friends? If I called, would they answer?*

My social media was no better. I had few followers because I didn't post much. I didn't know most of them in real life. None of them were people from Millerton, people I'd known as a kid. *Why did they all abandon me?*

The ridiculousness of that thought hammered me. I was the one who'd left. Without even giving them the courtesy of a goodbye.

I couldn't remember ever even searching through Facebook, Instagram, or Twitter for Xander. Or Sarah. Or anyone. Surely, I had at least once. Right?

I slowed down as I passed Sammy's Pub, the only bar I knew of in Miller County. A drink would taste good, but drinking alone seemed worse than just feeling sorry for myself.

I DROVE SLOWLY and carefully to avoid losing control like I had hours before. The sun rested above the ridges, ready to sink away for the night. The towering cornfields shimmered in the early-evening glow as I turned onto the gravel road.

I looked across the stalks waving in the Caldwells' field. The metal roof of their house glinted with a bright-orange reflection. Russ and Sarah were probably sitting down to dinner with their three kids. A happy and warm kitchen. Talking about the younger kids' games. Maybe discussing work around the farm. Perhaps having Harrison describe his time with me. Asking him questions about what we had discussed.

I hadn't expected Sarah to stay in Millerton. During those summers together growing up, we'd talked about what living in Charlotte was like. Shopping in glistening malls. Restaurants with fancy foods. Towering office buildings. Traffic and crowds.

During our senior year, when she was forced to live here, she'd shared her dreams about college and a career. None of it had involved staying here.

I was glad she'd found happiness here—she deserved it— but I couldn't figure out what changed for her. Three months after I left, she should have been settling into a dormitory and thinking of sororities and classes.

As I drove up our driveway, I vowed to patch things up with her as best I could before leaving this time. Even be nice to Russ for her. Most importantly, I would make a point of saying goodbye.

When I parked under the maple in our yard and shut off my engine, silence descended. I waited for the screen door to open. For Mom to appear on the porch. She'd heard me drive in. She must have. Nobody could come up that gravel road without being heard inside. She was probably watching from the shadows.

When she didn't emerge, I settled into one of the rocking chairs on the front porch and waited for her. The silence wrapped itself around me.

The noises of city life that I had become accustomed to

were missing. No screaming sirens, blaring car horns, or even the sound of jets taking off and landing from airports. The steady rumble of traffic and trains didn't fill the background. There wasn't a sidewalk within miles of the farm for a kid to ride a skateboard with the wheels clacking in the grooves. No stereos blasting from windows or neighbors fighting.

The longer I sat still, though, the more I heard. The constant hum of nature served as the backdrop. A fly buzzed lazily past my ear. Birds chittered in the swaying tree branches as leaves flapped in the gentle breeze. The distant creek gurgled behind the wall of corn.

The sounds of my childhood were drowned out in the city. Here, they surrounded and comforted me.

Despite my fear of returning, I surprised myself with pleasant memories of playing tag in these fields with Dean. How could I have been so miserable and ready to escape while also having so much fun?

Snippets of another memory surfaced. Dean racing his ATV through the rows of corn. In the next row, Russ straddling his own ATV, grinning and pushing the throttle wide-open. My skinny arms wrapped tightly around Dean's waist. Laughing as the wind flipped through my hair. Careening through the creek bed, slinging water high into the air. The engines roaring as we came up the other side of the bank, our clothes soaked and caked in mud.

We were maybe twelve or thirteen. Dean was already developing a teenaged musculature. The faintest hint of hair covered his upper lip. The scent of his sweat off his skin filled my nose. I, of course, was still trapped in the body of a little boy, waiting to catch up, as always.

Then the memory shifted. The happiness of the ride dwindled as my chest tightened with the looming signs of an impending allergy attack. The dust and dirt were choking off my lungs. I fought to breathe, gasping for precious oxygen.

Dean was racing the ATV again, the smile fading from his face as he pushed the ATV faster and faster. Russ followed, fighting to keep up and shouting to hurry. My arms were weakening. My body swayed. Dean gripped my hands, holding them together around his waist as he drove. He shouted at me to hold on, fear tinging his voice.

After bursting through the wall of corn and into the yard, the ATV skidded to a stop at the porch. The roar of the engine ceased. Dean jumped off the seat, scooped me up in his arms. He carried me up the porch steps as if I weighed no more than a bag of groceries.

The screen door slammed shut, then Dean's and Russ's boots clumped up the steps to the second floor. Mom's voice came from the kitchen, asking what was wrong.

Dean dropped me onto the bed, ripped open my top drawer, and extracted my inhaler—the one that was supposed to always be in my pocket when I left the house. He held it steady while I sucked in the relief.

Later that evening, as the sky outside my window purpled, I rested in bed, listening to the voices floating up the steps. In the back parlor, Dad asked Dean how he could have been so irresponsible. He demanded to know why Dean hadn't made sure I had my inhaler with me. Dean knew the dangers. Knew how I was always forgetful. How he was expected to look after me.

Dean didn't throw it back on me, though. He didn't argue that we were the same age. He didn't protest about the unfairness of being responsible for me.

No, I heard his voice clearly all these years later, saying the whole adventure was all his idea and that he was the one who'd forgotten to put the inhaler in the ATV's saddlebags.

Later still, I woke to find Dean sitting on the edge of my bed. It was pitch-black outside. When he saw I was awake, he asked if I'd had fun.

"Yes," I said. "Sorry you got into trouble."

He shrugged. "It was worth it."

My stomach rumbled. The sandwiches I'd eaten on this porch seemed farther in the past than just a few hours. I should have grabbed some food while in town, maybe fast food at one of the places out by the interstate. I doubted anything else had opened during my absence.

We'd rarely eaten at those places while growing up. Meals were Mom's cooking eaten around the kitchen table. Dean and I had shared clean-up duties.

I guessed Mom was still cooking for Dad, but what was she using? I'd already noted the decrepit state of the small garden behind the house. Had she canned enough fruits and vegetables the previous year? Or was she getting most of her food from the grocery store? When I was a kid, she'd prided herself in how little food she'd had to buy.

With all her focus on him, was she eating? In all my childhood memories, she was cooking, cleaning, or helping in the fields. She probably hadn't taken care of herself during Dad's illness. I should have offered to bring food home for her.

Opening the screen door, I called out for her, but I heard nothing in return. The sunlight filtering through the windows chased shadows, but she hadn't turned on any other lights. The kitchen was as dark as the front parlor.

I moved toward the rear parlor with a sense of dread, remembering not just the old memories of punishments being meted out but also the more recent scent of dying.

I slid open the pocket door and looked into the gloom. He lay on his back, head on a pillow and mouth sagging open. His face was pale, and his hands were crossed over his body. I was too late. He was gone. I licked my lips nervously and whispered, "Dad?"

"Come in." The voice startled me. Mom sat in the chair in the shadows of the corner, a light blanket draped over her lap. "He probably won't answer you. Evenings are hardest. He doesn't remember much then, barely recognizes me. You should come sit in the morning and talk with him."

"So he's…"

"Is he okay? No, but alive. For now." She folded closed a book she'd been reading with the help of the fading sunlight coming through the window. "I worry every night that he'll slip away while I'm asleep. I come in every couple of hours to check on him."

I looked over my shoulder at the steep steps to the second floor. Dean and I had slid down that banister more times than I could remember. "You're climbing up and down at night?"

She pointed toward the front parlor. "I sleep on the couch out there. Or in this chair. I don't want to be more than a few steps away in case he needs me. And I sure don't want him slipping away without me here."

I leaned against the doorframe, watching the sheets rise and fall gently with his breaths. "Have you had dinner?"

She shook her head.

"You want me to go into town and get you something?"

She settled the book on the small table and placed her reading glasses on the cover. Standing, she folded the blanket and placed it in the chair. Once everything was in its place, she motioned me to follow her. In the kitchen, she opened the refrigerator and gestured toward the rows of baking dishes wrapped in plastic wrap or aluminum foil or topped with plastic lids. "People stop by every day and leave more food than I could ever eat. Casseroles. Soups. Fresh eggs."

She selected a chicken casserole. While she waited for the oven to preheat, she extracted a crown of broccoli florets and two ears of corn. I shucked the corn, the muscle memory of youth helping me to cleanly remove the husks and silk.

With everything cooking, I stood in Dad's doorway and watched him. When the food was ready, we settled down at the kitchen table and ate while making small talk. Whenever he coughed or shifted in bed, she went into his room, checked on him, and returned.

After her fifth trip, she settled into her chair and held a fork over her half-eaten dinner. "Don't wait too late, Freddie."

"I'm here."

"Not what I meant." She placed the fork on the plate and leaned back in her chair, fixing me with a stare. "After breakfast, sit with him a spell. He's better in the mornings. He wants to spend time with you."

I snorted. "He called me Dean when I went in earlier. He wants him, not me."

"Of course he wants to see your brother. The other day, he thought I was his grandmother. He wanted her then, even though she's been gone for thirty years. I told you his mind gets confused."

"Ma, not just today. He's always wanted Dean more."

"Is that what you think?" She drummed her fingers on the table then pushed her chair back. "Wait here."

She disappeared into the shadows of the back parlor. I heard a cabinet door open, then she reappeared, holding a large scrapbook. She pushed my dinner to the side and slapped the book in front of me. "Open it."

I had seen it plenty of times growing up. The first pages had our birth certificates. Infant footprints. Our little hospital bracelets.

As I flipped through each sheet, the collage of photos showed us aging. Playing in the yard together. Wading in the creek. Sitting in a pew at church. At the dinner table.

Dean looked more like my older brother in every picture, not my twin. Taller and broader. Always looking at the camera, usually smiling. Exuding confidence while I looked down, my smiles forced when they appeared at all.

Then the pictures became less together and more separate. Dean wore sports uniforms. I sat at a piano. Dean on a tractor. Me on the porch with a book in my hand. Dean playing football. Me with an electric guitar. Separate fuzzy photos of us accepting our high school diplomas on the stage.

When I turned the page, I held my breath. Dean and I stood side-by-side in our graduation robes, holding up our diplomas. His arm was draped over my shoulder, a wide grin on his face. I was looking away from the camera, only the slightest smile on mine.

The memory flooded back to me. Dad holding his old camera and telling us to get closer. Mom beaming with pride. Dean laughing and whooping.

Taped to the opposite page was the church bulletin for Dean's funeral service, a stark reminder of how fast things had changed in those few days.

Before I turned the page, I asked, "Do you remember when Dean took me out on the ATV and I had an asthma attack?"

She smiled. "Which time?"

The memory that had floated through my mind. Had all the parts been the same day? Were we wearing the same clothes? Was the sun in the same place? Was the corn fully grown in some and already harvested in others? "The time he got into trouble for it and Dad yelled at him?"

She laughed. "Freddie, dear, that doesn't help much. It happened so many times. Dean took you on so many adventures he wasn't supposed to."

Flashes of other days came to mind. Fishing in the creek on cold spring mornings. Climbing the maple tree at the height of summer. Leaping out of the barn loft into a pile of freshly cut hay. "Why would he keep doing it if he was going to get into trouble?"

"We asked him the same question." She looked toward the back parlor, her head cocked, listening for any sounds that indicated she needed to go back in there. "Skeeter tried to explain that we were worried you'd get sick or hurt or worse. Dean argued you deserved to be a kid and have fun."

In my memories, we were always kids, no more than early teens. "So why'd he stop?"

She thought for a minute. "I don't know he ever really did, but life just got busy. School. Sports. Girls. Working here on the farm. There was just less time for either of you to be kids."

15

D ean's old room looked the same as it had the day I left. A dresser rested against one wall, the surface dusted and the drawers closed. A desk was tucked under the window, the chair pushed in tight. His bed was neatly made. If I lifted the mattress, would the *Playboy* magazines he used to hide still be there?

I opened the closet door and pulled the string to illuminate the overhead bulb. His Millerton High School letter jacket hung beside his football and baseball jerseys. Beside them, his favorite coat, a denim jacket lined with white fleece, stood out. He'd saved his allowance for months to buy it. I dragged my fingers over the coarse fabric, images flashing through my mind of the times I'd seen him wear it.

The rest of the rod held only a cluster of empty hangers. The overhead shelf was bare of baseball caps and winter gloves. No shoes lined the floor.

Most of the dresser drawers were equally empty. The T-shirts, underwear, socks, and shorts had all been taken away. All that remained were carefully folded uniform shirts, his baseball glove, and a cardboard box.

With the box in my hands, I sat on his bed and examined its contents. His old wallet sat on top. Inside it, I found his driver's license, library card, school ID, and seventeen dollars in cash. Below that was his key ring with a rabbit's foot attached. We'd always joked it wasn't lucky for the rabbit. The old white choker he used to like against his tanned neck was in the box, along with the tassel from high school graduation.

Those mementos bothered me more than the trophies. I could picture him so clearly. The denim jacket worn loosely, the fleece collar framing his face. That choker tight against his skin, glistening like his teeth. His hand proudly holding up his truck keys, that rabbit's foot dangling beside the class ring on his hand.

Mom—maybe Dad, but probably just Mom—had packed all the things that didn't matter, the nondescript pieces of clothing that any boy might wear. She'd hauled them to the church bazaar or maybe to the Goodwill store so she wouldn't have to witness their new owners carry them out the door.

What remained was quintessential Dean—things that marked him for who he was. The room wasn't really his any longer. It was a tribute to his memory. A museum.

Nothing said that more than the homemade shelves mounted on one wall displaying the rows of trophies and ribbons he'd earned over the years. Football. Baseball. Wrestling. The oldest was a small plastic football player from his first year in the Mighty Mites league. Seven years old and already beating kids two years older on the field. Everyone else reached for participation awards. Dean wanted to win.

Dad had cheered him on through every game, applauded at awards banquets, and glowed as he helped Dean build those shelves. Just further proof that Dean was the favored child.

Leaving our doors open, I crossed the hall and stretched out on my bed. From that vantage point, I could see his wall of honor, taunting me even now. The awards flaunted his athletic prowess and reminded me how little I had. Dad had never built me a trophy wall because I'd never earned any trophies.

Back then, my room was messy and disorganized, a chaos I preferred. Today, though, it was as neat and orderly as Dean's always had been. The closets and drawers were empty because I had taken it all with me. My leather jacket hung alone, my suitcase on the barren shelf.

I rolled off the bed and lifted the mattress. Twelve-year-old me had been lying in bed sick one afternoon when Dean crossed the hall with one of his precious magazines hidden away in his shirt. He was, of course, already well into puberty, while I still waited. He'd given it to me as a gift for me to pass the time and coached me how to hide it so Mom wouldn't find it. She'd obviously found it in the intervening years, because nothing was there.

I settled into the chair, touching the scrapbook that lay open on my desk to the funeral bulletin. Under the light cast from my old desk lamp, I read the words I couldn't bring myself to look at so many years ago. The order of the hymns. The schedule of prayers. The recession as I struggled under the weight of that casket.

I flipped the page of the scrapbook to be confronted by a photograph of the graffiti rock in front of the high school, emblazoned with Dean's name. A clipped article from the local newspaper came next, highlighting his sporting prowess and mourning Millerton's loss of a young son. More glowing accolades filled the next several sheets.

Then I flipped a page and came upon a yellowed sheet of paper with a newspaper article from the *San Antonio Express-News* reviewing a band's performance at a local club. My name was highlighted. It wasn't the original article from the newspaper but printed on a sheet of paper, cut out, and taped to the page with a handwritten note beside it. *Freddie's band.*

I knew that scrawl well. I'd grown up seeing it in the ledger downstairs in the office. Or on lists of supplies scribbled on a pad in the barn. The handwriting was Dad's, not Mom's.

Other articles followed. Nashville. Dallas. Denver. Los Angeles. Chicago. Interviews and mentions I'd never read. Shows I didn't even remember.

The scrapbook didn't capture every show I'd ever done, of course. Most weren't newsworthy enough to be mentioned in any newspaper, much less ones that he would have had access to through the local library. Some articles wouldn't have even mentioned me, just the name of the band.

I stared at the ceiling, trying to recall all of the band names. Some of the stints had been very brief. The band had broken up, or I'd left before it could. If I couldn't think of them all, there was no way anyone else would know them.

But Dad had collected dozens of articles. For a man who didn't relish leaving the farm, that was lots of local library time before the internet came to the farm.

One interview mentioned me earning my nickname in a bar fight. The words *Mad Maverick* were written in the margin. It was underlined with a note that read, *That's what he calls himself now.* After that were pages mentioning Mad Maverick, including some written before that interview. He had apparently searched for the name and found other articles.

Then came Exploding Oatmeal. Article after article about the band. Most of the ones I knew of were focused on the lead singer, but Dad had left those out. He'd kept only the ones that mentioned me or had a photo of me—in the background, of course.

When I reached the end of the book, I found a map taped to the inside cover. I unfolded it and stared at the highlights. He had taken the tour dates mentioned in the articles and noted the cities I had been in with the year scribbled beside them. My finger traced the highways and paused over the cities he'd noted, mostly obscure places I couldn't even recall. A mall, a small stage, a festival—they all blurred together in my memory.

Then my finger froze over one note. *Asheville. 2019. So close.*

We had played the Orange Peel in downtown. A grand show with a raucous crowd. We'd needed to be in Atlanta the next night, and I'd told myself I didn't have time to rent a car and drive the half hour over to Millerton.

I closed the book and stared out the window.

16

The smell of biscuits baking and coffee percolating wafted up the steps and gently nudged me from my sleep. The hint of sunrise poked through the open window. A crow in a nearby tree cawed and was answered by a chorus of his mates.

Sleep had come slowly. I'd lain in bed with the lights out, listening to the lonely hoot of an owl in the rafters of the barn. A creak in the house had brought back memories of Dean sneaking in late at night, tiptoeing across the porch roof, and opening his bedroom window. I listened in vain for the clump of his shoes as he dropped into his room.

When I couldn't stand another minute, I'd turned on the lamp on my bedside table, pulled on my jeans and sweatshirt, and retrieved the scrapbook from my desk. I'd stretched across the bed, going through it again and again. I'd fallen asleep, still dressed, on top of the covers while flipping through the pages. Now it lay open beside me.

After a quick shower, I dressed in clean clothes—another pair of black jeans and a T-shirt—and opened the window blinds. The sun peeked over the horizon. The yard below still rested in shadows.

I rubbed my eyes and reached for my phone. It wasn't quite six o'clock. I was more accustomed to going to bed at such a time, not waking up. The old early-morning habits of farm life were foreign to me now.

I leaned against the window frame and yawned. A few high wisps of clouds danced across the clear blue sky. The leaves of the maple flipped in the morning breeze. I shivered and reached for the sweatshirt I'd bought the day before.

Following my nose, I stumbled down the steps and entered the kitchen. I found a mug in a cabinet—where they'd been for as long as I could remember—and poured myself a cup of coffee. As I leaned against the counter and sipped the magic elixir, Mom bustled into the room. "Good morning, sleepyhead."

"Let me guess. You've been up for at least an hour."

She pointed at the counter. "Someone had to gather the fresh eggs from the chickens. Used to be your job. Do you want them scrambled or fried? Grits and biscuits are cooking, and I've got bacon."

"Already slaughter a pig this morning?"

"Store-bought. Sorry to disappoint."

"No, of course not. It's just…" I struggled to explain how things had changed for me. As kids, we'd eaten whatever was put in front of us, or we did without. "I don't normally eat like this for breakfast."

"What do you eat? Or do you even get up for breakfast?"

I opted not to answer the second question. Explaining a musician's late nights and subsequent late starts to the day was more than I was ready to tackle. Besides, I reasoned, breakfast was the first meal of the day, even if the day started after noon. "I usually just have some fruit when I get up."

She paused with her hands on her hips, her lips pursed in thought. "Too early for apples, but we've got some fresh strawberries. Good crop this year."

"That'd be perfect."

"Good. I'll get them ready while you chat with Skeeter."

I froze. Discussing the hours I kept with my mother was scary enough. Talking to Dad was a whole different level. "He's awake?"

"I told you. He's better in the mornings. Go talk, and I'll have your breakfast waiting when you're done."

To my surprise, I'd already drained my first cup of coffee. I refilled it and carried it into the rear parlor.

THE WINDOW WAS open a few inches, and a fresh, cool breeze wafted in. The golden hues of the morning sunlight filtered through the sheers, chasing the shadows out of the corners. I could hear songbirds cheerfully greeting the morning. The vibrance of life just outside the window seemed out of place with the dying in the room.

Dad's eyes fluttered open and locked onto me as I entered the room. He motioned for me to sit in the chair beside the bed. "Libby tells me I called you Dean yesterday. Sorry about that."

"It's okay, Dad."

"It's just that I see him a lot lately. In my head, I mean. At least, I think it's in my head. That morphine does a job on your mind." He shifted on the bed, a bony rustling under the covers. "Not just him. My parents. My sister. Old friends. It's like they're waiting for me."

I looked at the shadows congregating in the corners of the room and wondered if they watched from just outside my vision. Dean had loved telling ghost stories, but it'd made for many a sleepless night as I warily guarded against evil spirits after the lights went out. It seemed strange to me that they could be a source of comfort.

Dad brought me back to the present by saying, "Right now, though, I need to talk to the living. So I'm sorry I called you Dean yesterday."

I didn't know how to respond. I couldn't remember him ever apologizing to me about anything. I sat in stunned silence and waited.

After a pregnant pause, he continued, "So, tell me about you. Still playing in bands?"

When had Dad ever asked about bands and music? Haltingly at first, I told him about how I felt on stage, lost in the music and the cheering of a crowd. I explained how Exploding Oatmeal was right on the cusp of a world tour when the randomness of Covid snatched it away. He listened, nodding and his eyes bright as I painted the picture of the other band members. His slight smile hinted he could see the band and feel our excitement for the tour. The shake of his head showed he shared my distaste for the lead singer and his overbearing ways. He grumbled when I told him about finding out a replacement had stepped into my spot on the stage.

I'd never thought he would been interested at all, but that scrapbook suggested something different. The way he listened to my tales confirmed it.

When I finished, we lapsed into a comfortable silence. I thought he had drifted off to sleep. Then his eyes fluttered open, and he focused on my face. I couldn't remember him ever looking so directly at me. "So what's next? What are you doing now?"

"I play whenever and wherever I can."

His eyes narrowed. "Are you having fun?"

The question threw me more than the apology had. I wasn't sure I could answer it. I hadn't put much thought into it, but doubts swirled. When was music last fun? I tried to speak but could only shrug in response.

Dad's hand slid out from under the blanket and gripped my

wrist. The fingers were warmer than they had been the day before. "Life's short, son. I sure know that. And Dean does. You gotta have fun. Promise me that."

"Did..." I hesitated, not sure I wanted to ask—or should. Dad, though, looked at me intently, so I plunged ahead. "Did you have fun?"

A smile spread over his gaunt face. His hand released its grip. "Being out in those fields under the summer sun, walking rows of crops, fixing a broken fence—nothing made me happier. Except your mother, of course. And both my sons. So, yes, I was doing exactly what I wanted to do with my life."

"Just like Dean."

The smile faltered. "I hope. Sometimes, I worried he was just doing it because he thought I expected him to."

"Didn't you?"

Silence haunted the room. I worried I had pushed too far. I wanted to take the question back, but I was also curious what the response was. Skeeter replied quietly. "Yes. I always just assumed he would."

"But not me."

The smile returned, though more wistful than before. "No, not you. I always knew you were going to leave. You did your chores and everything you were supposed to, but this life wasn't for you."

"And that disappointed you?"

"Not for one second." Skeeter closed his eyes, and his head sank back into the pillow. With a sigh, he continued in a hushed voice. "That's not true. Time's too short for lies. Truth is, yes, I was disappointed. For a bit."

That stung. I leaned back in the chair, not knowing how to respond. He saved me by continuing, "Growing up, I itched to leave this place and go out into the world, just like you always did. A few years in the army cured that curiosity. I came back with my tail between my legs, but your pappy took me in like I'd never been gone. He said he always knew I'd return."

"And you thought we'd do the same?"

"Dean, yes. I figured he'd go sow his wild oats and then show up on the doorstep someday." Breath wheezed in and out. The conversation had zapped the little energy he had. He was fading. "But not you. By the time you were ten or twelve, I knew you'd leave forever."

"I was barely playing guitar then."

"Not as a musician. I didn't know that yet." He turned his head sideways so he could look me in the eye. "Just that you'd go do something else."

"And that bothered you?"

"At first. But then…" He shrugged.

"What changed?"

A snicker slipped from him. It sent him into a coughing fit. I grabbed the glass off the table and held the straw so he could get a sip of water. When he'd recovered, he said, "Your mother told me to get over it."

"And so you just did?"

"How did defying your mother ever work for you?"

It was my turn to laugh. "Not well."

"Nor for me, son. Nor for me." His eyes slipped shut again. He was fading back to sleep. "As always, though, she was right, so I just accepted it. Scared the bejesus out of me, but I accepted it."

"Scared?" I couldn't fathom him being scared of anything other than not getting a good harvest. "Why did it scare you?"

He slid his tongue across his lips. "I was scared I'd never see you again."

His fear had almost come true. If it had been left just to me, it would have. I would never have returned if my mother hadn't called and told me to. I leaned forward and clasped my hands over his. My voice breaking, I said, "I'm here now. I'm glad I came."

Only soft snoring answered.

17

When I returned to the kitchen, Mom ushered me to the table and placed a bowl of sliced strawberries with a dollop of whipped cream in front of me. Then she added a plate filled with scrambled eggs, grits, bacon, and fluffy biscuits. When I tried to protest, she retrieved a jar of honey harvested from their hive behind the barn and slipped it into my hand.

Some people thought eating a spoonful of local honey to keep allergies at bay was an old wives' tale. As she always joked, she was an old wife, so she knew the truth. She had been giving me honey since before I could walk.

Besides, I had a sweet tooth, so she had her secret weapon. She knew I couldn't resist. I didn't.

I started with a few bites of strawberries. Then I slathered butter onto the biscuits and poured that thick honey on top. I bit into the warm fluffiness dripping with sweet. My eyes closed in delight as I savored the flavor exploding over my tongue.

With my appetite whetted, it didn't take me long to dive into everything. A forkful of eggs was followed with homemade grits, nothing like the lumpy, store-bought instant. Besides, I knew from watching her cook when I was a child that her secret sauce was a jar of fat drippings kept near the stove for flavoring. The chomp of bacon ended the last of my resistance. I ate like I'd been rescued from a deserted island.

She had learned to cook from her mother and grand-mother. Preparing meals for Dad had always been easy. He came in from a hard day of work, hungry and ready for what-ever she put in front of him. Dean, with his ravenous appetite, had been just as simple to please.

Me? I'd challenged her. In my early days when I had been so sickly, I often tried to skip meals. She'd never forced me to eat but always tempted me with flavors and smells.

She traded recipes at church. When in town, she would swing by the library and check the magazines for meal ideas. She wasn't bragging when she said she went from being a good cook to a superb one just to please my picky palate. In the years I'd been away, I'd forgotten the joy of a home-cooked meal.

When people asked what it was like being a musician, I would brag that we ate in fancy restaurants. I didn't want to admit that truck stops were as good as it got, although many of them were pretty good. More often, though, it was bland fast food. Or worse, day-old bread and sandwich meats on sale at a discount grocery as their expiration dates loomed. More than once, I'd made a meal of stale pretzels from a bar because I didn't have any cash.

After several minutes of gluttony, I mopped the last tasty morsel off my plate. I leaned back in my chair and stared at the empty plate in front of me, surprised at how much I'd eaten. The smile on her face and the twinkle in her eyes suggested Mom wasn't.

I OFFERED to help clean the dishes, but she shooed me out of the kitchen to the front porch. She suggested I wait in a rocking chair and enjoy the fresh morning air. She assured me she would join me to talk when she was done.

I stood at the top of the steps and stretched. As stuffed as I was, I would have fallen asleep if I'd followed her directions. My eyes drifted around the yard and settled on the flower beds. Memories of my childhood chores bubbled up in my mind. At the time, I'd thought of them as drudgery, a necessary task to complete so I could move on to something more fun.

But I also remembered the satisfaction in seeing the fruition of my work. A little sweat produced an obvious result. And since the work was so rote, so mindless, my thoughts would pick at a composition I'd been working on. How many songs had I written while plucking unwanted plants from her gardens?

I found myself descending the steps to the flower beds and dropping to my hands and knees. I pulled weeds without thinking about it. The cobwebbed memories came back to me, how to grab each growth as low as possible so I could pull it out by the root. The pile of weeds beside me grew as I worked to expose the flowers.

After some time had passed, the screen door squeaked open and slammed shut. Mom's coffee mug clinked as she settled it on the table and descended the steps to join me. Without a word, we worked side by side, clearing her flower beds.

The June sun rose in the sky and warmed the morning. Between it and the steady work, sweat broke out on my body. I stripped off my sweatshirt and hung it from the porch railing. I felt her eyes studying the tattoos running up my exposed arms, but I focused on my task.

The flowers were increasingly unmolested in their soil. We

gathered the detritus and dumped it into a bucket she'd retrieved before moving to the next section.

Finally, she broke the silence. "Did you have a good chat with your father?"

I rocked back on my knees and studied her. My suspicions said she'd stood just outside the door and listened. She'd probably suggested what he should say. It certainly was out of character for him.

Then I decided it didn't matter if she had encouraged him. After all, she had encouraged me. No matter the impetus, the conversation felt more real than any we'd ever had. "I wanted to ask him about the scrapbook."

"Maybe tomorrow."

We returned to work and settled back into the old routine of my childhood—exchanging a few words, passing some time in silence, and resuming the conversation again. It was less awkward than the day before. I felt more able to say what I thought to her, just as I had as a kid. "He never paid much attention to my music when I was growing up."

"Not true. He went to your talent shows at school."

I chuffed. "That's because you made him."

"Not true." She avoided my accusing look. "Well, not totally. But he bought you that guitar for your thirteenth birthday."

That stopped my work. I sat on my haunches, a dandelion dangling from my fingers. I loved the acoustic guitar that Anna had given me, but I'd wanted to go electric as I entered my teens. She'd had one hanging on the wall in her store. I'd been allowed to take it down a few times and play it, but she couldn't afford not to sell it to a paying customer. "I thought that was you."

She smiled. "Every time we went to town, you had to go by there and look at it again."

"I wanted it so bad."

"I know. I wanted to buy it for you myself, but times were tight. I told Skeeter about it one evening. He went down the next day to haggle over it with Anna." She laughed. "You should have heard him squawking about how much it cost, but it didn't matter. He was determined to get it for you. It was a present from both of us, but he bought it."

I remembered the day I walked into the store and stared at the empty spot on the wall. I'd tried to feign happiness for Anna as she wished me a happy birthday, but all I could think of was that someone else had the guitar I wanted.

When I arrived home that evening and mounted the stairs, Dean showed off the new baseball glove Dad had bought him. I opened the door to my own room and froze. The guitar lay on my bed, adorned with a giant red ribbon. The small amp rested on the floor.

Dean looked over my shoulder and exclaimed, "Cool."

I picked it up and played a few chords. Then I raced down the steps, threw my arms around my mother's neck, and cried, "Thank you. Thank you. Thank you."

My father had watched from behind his desk in the rear parlor, never saying a word about his involvement.

"I never knew." I focused on my work. My pride grew when I saw the results. The simple pleasure of working in the dirt soothed and relaxed me. "Why didn't he tell me?"

"Because your father's never been good at talking about things."

"He talked to Dean all the time."

She chewed on her lip. "About the farm. Sports. Surface stuff."

"But he never talked to me about those things."

"Because you weren't interested in farming or sports."

I let loose a deep exhale of frustration. "I never understood why it was so easy for the two of them. It's like they had something special between them I didn't have."

Mom stood and brushed the dirt off her knees. She motioned for me to join her on the porch. "Let me tell you something."

18

I thought I knew the story. How Dean was born forty-two minutes before me. He was healthy, and I wasn't. But I didn't know the details. Dean was born a full pound and a half bigger than me. He exited the womb healthy and strong, ready to command the world. His cries filled the delivery rooms. The nurse cooed over him. Mom watched Skeeter hold him, beaming with pride.

Minutes later, the jubilant atmosphere in the room grew somber. Smiles slipped from the faces of the doctor and nurse. A quick call brought reinforcements, and others crowded in, people she had never met. A nurse snatched Dean from Skeeter's arms so he could hold Mom's hand. He did his job, reassuring her that everything would be okay, but she could see the truth in his eyes. They were filled with worry.

When I slid into the world a few minutes later, just after midnight, I didn't cry or scream. I didn't make any sound at all. The doctor snipped the umbilical cord, and a nurse whisked me from the room before Mom could even see me.

The doctor tried to reassure them. They had neonatal

specialists working on me, he said. The team was excellent. I was in capable hands.

The more he tried to act like everything was okay, the less she believed. She and Dad clung to each other, hoping and praying. They took turns holding Dean, but they worried.

An hour or two later—though it seemed like an eternity to them—a neonatologist came into the room and introduced himself. With tears in his eyes, Dad held Dean close to his chest and paced the room as the doctor patiently described the issues. Mom's head spun in confusion. She remembered only snippets. Struggling to breathe. Currently residing in NICU. Neonatal intensive care unit. Great staff. Round-the-clock care. But…

They wanted to move me to Mission Hospital in Asheville. "Just a precaution," he assured them, but they thought it would be for the best. "Probably be there for a week. Maybe two. Hopefully not three. But…"

Another but.

The specialist lowered his voice and warned that things were touch and go. "We're doing everything we can," he assured them, "but…"

My mother, who was always calm and unflappable, wanted to scream and throw things. She knew the words he was going to say and didn't want to hear them, but he said it anyway. "Sometimes, everything we can do isn't enough."

He left the room. They sat quietly, with Dean's gurgling and chirping the only sounds in the room. They absorbed the conversation in their silence, not wanting to say the words out loud, but they understood. I might not survive.

She grabbed my hand at that point in the story and squeezed. "How does a mother deal with a healthy newborn and an infant at death's door at the same time? I wanted to cradle and nurture Dean. As exuberant as he was, he was still an infant. My son. He needed mothering. But you needed me more."

With the words "might not survive" echoing in her brain, she mapped out a strategy with Dad. As much as she hated to be separated from Dean, she knew she needed to be with me.

And as much as Dad wanted to be with me, they couldn't bring Dean to the hospital in Asheville. That was far too dangerous for an infant. Besides, he wouldn't be allowed in the NICU. Divide and conquer was the only answer.

Dad vowed to handle everything with Dean at home. Feedings. Changing diapers. Everything. She trusted he would. She had to. She had no other choice.

For the next few weeks, she rose before the sun each morning, made sure enough breast milk was on hand to feed Dean, kissed her one son goodbye for the day, then left for the long drive to Asheville to be with her other son. She sat with me in that sterile NICU department until late each evening. Reluctantly, she would leave me in the nurses' capable hands and drive home to sit with Dean until she fell asleep. Dad would take him from her arms and get him resettled in his crib before guiding her to bed.

As exhausted as she was, she never asked Dad how he balanced running the farm and caring for Dean. In those critical early weeks of May, though, he had things that needed doing. Farming didn't wait for sick babies. The truth came out only after I finally came home.

Dad, by then, had become quite accustomed to handling Dean's needs. Like in everything else in life, he was an easy baby. Sleeping when he was supposed to and suckling bottles without complaint. He was even somewhat predictable about soiling his diapers.

Not me, of course. My fussiness nearly overwhelmed them. Mom struggled to get me to eat and sleep. She had planned to spend more time with Dean when I came home, but I demanded most of her attention. She didn't object when Dad came into the nursery to help.

One morning, when I was worse than even my terrible normal, Dad offered to take Dean out of the room. He bundled the healthier boy up in blankets, just like he had every other morning during her absence. Before Mom realized what was happening, Dad had him settled in a wicker basket and carried out the back door.

Shocked, Mom ran after him and demanded to know what he was doing. "The same thing I've done every other morning," he explained. He carried Dean down to the barn.

When Mom gasped, he clarified he made sure Dean stayed warm and dry while he tended to his chores. The boy was never out of his sight. He changed Dean's diaper when needed. His feedings were timely. The barn was as warm and comfortable as the house in the spring air. The care was exactly the same as if the two of them stayed inside the house. To Dad, it made perfect sense.

Not to Mom, though. She was horrified. They argued, but ultimately, she had to admit that Dean was no worse for wear. He was healthy and happy. Dad was very attentive. She simply forbade the dangerous behavior in the future.

Until my first cold came along. Then my second. And then my third. Unlike Dean, I caught every bug that floated through the air. Mom took me to the doctor's office frequently.

Dad had to keep the farm running if they wanted to have enough money for food, utilities, and the mounting medical bills. With her hands full and at her wit's end on how to balance everything, Mom reluctantly agreed to let Dad take Dean to the barn so he wouldn't catch my germs. She wore a path walking back and forth between the house and the barn, checking on me and making sure Dad was watching Dean.

Over time, she relaxed. The arrangement became natural.

I spent my first few years in the house with Mom. Dad watched Dean for many hours in the barn.

Dean crawled first. Walked first. Spoke first. He toddled about the yard with abandon, playing in the dirt under Dad's watchful eyes while I stayed inside, away from pollen and everything that made me sneeze. Dad never minded taking Dean when Mom needed to watch me. Dean seemed to thrive on the treatment.

One day when Dean and I were three, she looked out the window and saw Dean sitting in Dad's lap as he piloted the tractor through the field. She headed for the door to ask him exactly what the hell he was thinking when the sound of me banging on the piano keys stopped her.

Her old upright sat at the end of the front parlor. She rarely had time to play, so it gathered dust. I knelt on the bench and tapped the keys with my little fingers. Not chords. Not Mozart. I was no prodigy. But notes. Simple notes. Strung together.

She stood mesmerized in the kitchen doorway as I experimented. My head cocked as I listened to my own production. Forgetting Dean on the big John Deere, she settled onto the bench beside me.

That was the first day of a long tradition. Each afternoon after lunch, the two of us sat side by side, playing notes and basic chords while Dean hung out with Dad. By the time I entered school, I was practicing scales and simple songs while Dean handed tools to Dad as he fixed the tractor. On weekends, Dad and Dean would go fishing in the creek while I learned a concerto. Dad offered to take me, too, but I preferred my music.

I LEANED against the support column on the porch and picked dirt from under my nails. "He actually thought it was a good idea to take an infant to a barn?"

She laughed. "You've been citified too much. I wasn't so worried about the barn as being sure your father would keep his focus on Dean. You know how he gets when he's working."

My shock must've shown on my face, because she shook her head and continued, "You have to remember how differently he and I were raised. Skeeter barely finished high school. That was only because his father never did and wouldn't let him quit. Your great-grandfather only went a few years to school at all. Before that, who knows? Most McDougals probably never saw the inside of a schoolhouse. Kids grew up working on the farms. It's just what was expected."

"But it was dangerous. Kids died doing that."

"Of course. No one is okay with that, of course, but it was just part of it. I was collecting eggs from the chickens by the time I was four. Trust me, chickens would peck a kid's hand as fast as an adult's, but you learned from it."

"But—"

"If Dean had lived, don't you think he'd have your nieces or nephews doing chores around the farm?"

I sat back down in the chair beside her. The thought of Dean with kids made me melancholy. He had volunteered in high school to coach some of the youth sports in town. Like everything else, he was good at it. The kids adored him. "Yeah, he probably would."

"I'm not asking you to approve of how your father and I handled things. We made plenty of mistakes." She patted my hand. "Just understand what we did and why we did it. It's how we were raised and who we are."

I closed my eyes and nodded. "I get it. He was closer to Dean because he spent more time with him in those first few years."

"It was never intentional. It just happened."

"But that means he probably wishes it was me in that wreck and not Dean."

She grabbed me and wagged a finger with her free hand. "Don't you dare say that. He loves you both. He'd never wish harm on you."

I looked over the fields. "I didn't mean it to come out that way. It's just that he raised Dean to take over the farm. Without him…"

She rocked and nodded. "It certainly has been harder than we'd dreamed."

I hesitated, wanting to ask a question but knowing it might hurt. Finally, I couldn't keep it quiet any longer. "Were you angry at Dean?"

"For the accident?"

I nodded.

"I suppose. Some. Maybe that's natural."

"I meant…" I looked away, avoiding her eyes. "I meant for being drunk."

"Oh, honey." She squeezed my arm. "Dean wasn't drunk."

Of course he was drunk. Everyone knew that. Why deny it? "Why else would he drive off a road?"

Her eyes welled up with tears. "He was sober. The autopsy confirmed it."

My head swam in confusion. "But…?"

She leaned back in her chair and told me what she knew.

19

The knock that came at the door that Sunday morning still echoed in my brain. For a brief second, I wondered who could possibly visit at such a strange time, but I had my own problems to focus on.

How was I going to hide my swollen eye from Mom? She hated it when Dean and I fought. As mad as I was at him for chatting with Sarah, I didn't want to get him into trouble.

I listened for stirring from his room but heard nothing. He'd probably been out partying with Blake and spent the night over there. When he did that, though, he tried to sneak in before sunrise to avoid getting caught.

Twice, our parents had already called up the steps to see if we were getting dressed for church. A graduation party the night before was no excuse for us to skip. If anything, it was more a reason we had to go. No telling what sins we had committed out of their sight. If Dean wasn't back yet—and the lack of answering from his room said that was probably true—things would be tense around the house.

And now the knock suggested we had a neighbor with loose

cattle or coyote troubles. The sound of the front door opening drifted up the steps. Then my mother wailed.

I jumped out of bed, pulled on a pair of sweat pants, and clambered down the steps just in time to see my father slump to the floor in shock. A uniformed deputy stood at the door, clutching his hat in his hands. He looked up at me, but I didn't want to hear what he had to say.

Instead, I raced back up the stairs and pushed open the door to Dean's room. The trophies lined the shelves above his desk. Notebooks from the just-completed year were stacked on the corner of the desk. The cover on his bed was neatly tucked, not slept in the night before.

I turned, ran across the hall, and slammed my door shut behind me. I stayed there, crying and moaning in grief, until the sunlight faded. The first day without Dean in the world ended. I hadn't thought I would ever eat again, but I surprised myself by realizing I was hungry. I slipped down the steps on bare feet.

Mom looked up from her old wingback chair in the front parlor, her eyes red and puffy. When she saw the bruise on the side of my head, her eyes widened. I braced myself to explain, but she didn't want to know. Instead, she asked, "Want me to fix you some dinner?"

A plethora of casseroles lined the counter. The grief machine of Miller County was in full swing. I had spent enough time indoors growing up, so I knew my way around a kitchen. "I'll warm something."

Normally, she would have insisted. She prided herself on keeping things in the McDougal house organized. Instead, she stared at the wadded tissue in her hand and nodded.

My father, slumped in his desk chair in the rear parlor, never looked up. I selected the closest casserole I saw. I didn't think I could taste a thing, so didn't care about the contents.

After I stuck it into the oven to warm, I leaned against the sink near the open window.

On the front porch, neighbors sat in rocking chairs, talking in low voices. Snippets of their conversations floated through the window.

"What a tragedy."

"Poor Libby without her son."

"How can Skeeter keep things running without Dean's help?"

"Crops need tending, and they can't wait."

"Freddie is going to have to put down his silly guitar, roll up his sleeves, and learn to farm."

In my grief, I hadn't thought about what would happen next. Were they right? Would I be forced to give up my dreams? My plan to leave Millerton at the end of the summer got accelerated.

For the next two days, I stayed in my room and packed my clothes in an old duffel bag I'd found tucked away in Dean's closet, something he'd used to carry equipment to practice over the years. It smelled of his sweat, but I didn't mind.

I rarely left my room and spoke with almost no one. Not Sarah. Not Xander. Certainly none of Dean's friends who streamed in and out of the house. My parents busied themselves with funeral arrangements and greeting the many visitors stopping by with their condolences.

A detective from the sheriff's department visited me with questions. When did I last see Dean? What did we say to each other? What caused the fight? Who else was there?

I said as little as I could. The fight was typical sibling rivalry, nothing else. The last I'd seen of Dean was him driving away from the graduation party. After that, I'd come home and fallen asleep. I didn't know anything else.

I wasn't trying to avoid talking to them. At least, no more than I ever avoided talking to anyone. Besides, what difference did it make? What I was doing when Dean crashed didn't matter.

He asked my parents questions too. My mother assured the deputy that she knew I was home. She didn't, of course. She hadn't seen me come home. We never spoke that night.

I never wondered why the deputies asked where I was that night. In my grief and rage, I had assumed the accident had been wholly Dean's fault. It had all been a stupid accident. I didn't want to dwell on it.

But knowing Dean wasn't drunk changed everything. Questions I should have asked in the first place exploded.

WHILE DAD SLEPT, Mom quietly searched through the desk drawers for a copy of the accident report. She came back onto the porch and plopped into her chair empty-handed. "I can't find it. Maybe he shredded it. He threatened to often enough."

My stomach knotted in frustration. She had tried to explain to me what the report said, but I wanted to read it for myself. "Why would he get rid of it?"

She looked out toward the horizon. "When they told us about the autopsy, it about destroyed us. We were happy he hadn't been drunk, but then the whole accident made less sense. We read and reread the report, but that made it even harder to accept. And the pictures..."

I swallowed. "You saw accident photos?"

She shook her head. "I couldn't. They had them, but I didn't want to see. But Skeeter..."

"Dad saw them."

She nodded and wiped tears off her face. "Only a few. Then he had to stop. It crushed him."

"What did the reports say?"

When she couldn't bring herself to answer, I used my

phone to pull up the highway patrol's website. As I suspected, accident reports were online, but the available records didn't go back seventeen years. I needed to find out how long it would take to get physical copies. I was searching for the phone number for the local office when Mom stopped me.

"I've got a better idea." She called the sheriff's office and asked if they could help get the information from the state. The sergeant who'd answered the phone offered to see what he could find. He promised to call my cell as soon as he had an answer.

Within an hour, my phone rang. When I put it on speaker, we were both surprised. "This is Sheriff David Newman." Another advantage of a small, rural county.

After a few pleasantries, I explained how Mom thought he might be able to help me get copies of Dean's accident report from the highway patrol. His answer was better than I had expected.

He explained they had investigated the accident jointly with the highway patrol. The patrol had jurisdiction for the traffic accident, so they took the lead. The sheriff's office, though, had been on scene first and had the local knowledge and manpower to talk to people who had seen Dean the night before. "The good news is that means we have copies of the files here in our office. If you give me an hour or so, I can have our files pulled and confirm with them that they don't have anything additional. Then come on down, and I'll review it all with you."

So I cleaned up and headed into town.

As I PASSED the cemetery on the way into town, I slowed and noticed the church parking lot was empty. After avoiding Dean's grave for so many years, it made no sense to visit twice in two days, but it drew me in. A quick check of my watch told me I needed to take some time to give the sheriff a full hour.

Coming home had stirred up so many memories and feelings I'd thought I had buried long ago. In the brief time I had been back in Miller County, though, I'd started to question whether I really remembered correctly.

Not just whether Dean was drunk. At least I had an excuse for not knowing that. I saw him leave with his buddies, friends he would toss back a few beers with. And he'd spent the night at Blake's, the place he always went when he'd been out drinking and didn't want our parents to find out. My assumption had been logical.

But what about taking me riding on his ATV? Getting into trouble for it and refusing to throw me under the bus? Sneaking me magazines he wasn't even supposed to have? Even jumping to my defense when Blake and his friends bullied me? Photos on his wall of the two of us together?

I sat on the grass beside his headstone, absentmindedly tracing the letters spelling out beloved brother.

What really happened that night?

20

S hortly before noon, I sat at a table opposite Sheriff Newman. He hadn't been the sheriff when Dean's accident occurred, and I didn't ever remember meeting him, but he seemed to know who I was. Or at least, he knew who Dean was. He'd worked security for some of the high school football games back when he was a deputy.

So, once again, I was Dean's brother.

"I didn't work the accident. Heard about it, of course. Such a tragedy." He patted the folder sitting on the table in front of him. "When you called, I pulled the file and scanned the notes. Thought it might be good if we chatted about it, if you're sure you want to see it."

He wore blue jeans and a flannel shirt, not a uniform or suit. I wondered if he always dressed like that. Maybe it was his good-old-boy approach to make people forget he carried a gun and wore a badge. Or maybe it was his day off. But why he would come in on his day off to talk about an old accident, I didn't know.

My leg bounced under the table, and I gripped my knee to make it stop. I hadn't realized I would be so nervous sitting in a police station. "I was surprised when you called. When we spoke to the desk sergeant, I thought maybe they would make a copy of it or something like that. I never expected to have you take up your time."

He folded his hands and leaned forward in his chair. "Unsolved cases haunt me."

"Unsolved? I thought it was an accident."

"Let's call it unexplained. No clear sign of what caused the accident." The sheriff kept his gaze steady, unblinking. "Can I ask what sparked your interest?"

I released my knee and wiped my sweaty palms on my jeans. I stared at the folder sitting on the table. Were they so organized that they could pull a seventeen-year-old accident report that quickly? I had no idea how they maintained records, but the movies never made it look that easy. "First time I've been home since high school. I had always thought Dean had been drinking. Mom just told me he wasn't."

The sheriff drummed his fingers on the folder in front of him, keeping his eyes locked on me. After a long pause, he opened the folder and flipped a few pages, searching for something. When he found the right page, his finger scanned the lines of the text then tapped a number. "Tests showed he wasn't drunk. Not close."

"But he had been drinking?"

"Based on interviews with his friends, they drank a couple of beers at Blake Torrence's house the night before. Early the next morning, Dean got up and drove home. He was under-aged and shouldn't have been drinking at all, but there was no sign that it caused the accident. Alcohol was ruled out as a factor."

I scratched the side of my head as I let that sink in. I'd heard my parents make excuses for Dean when he got into trouble. Just boys being boys. Kid stuff. Part of me had assumed Mom just wanted to believe Dean wasn't drunk. Now it was confirmed. "Then what was the cause?"

"Unfortunately, we never found anything definitive." The sheriff flipped back several pages in the file then spun it around to a drawing showing a two-lane road. "He came through this series of curves with no signs of trouble and entered the straight stretch heading east. About a half mile later, he went off the right side of the road and hit a tree. His car was found at 6:18 a.m. Based on that and the time of departure from the Torrence house, we believe he wrecked around six o'clock."

I'd always imagined people witnessing the wreck then offering aid and comfort. "So he wasn't discovered for almost a half hour?"

"Sunday morning. Rural stretch of road. The deputy who discovered the accident was coming from a call way out toward the county line. He didn't recall passing another vehicle on his way back into town."

I studied the drawing, imagining Dean sitting alone in the wreckage, waiting for someone to spot him. "No one saw anything?"

"Closest structure was this dairy barn." He tapped the drawing. "They were inside, milking cows. First they knew of the accident is when they heard the highway patrol and fire truck arriving on scene."

"They didn't hear the wreck?"

"One of the guys said he thought he heard skidding, but he wasn't sure. Figured it was maybe kids hot-rodding, though that didn't make much sense for a Sunday morning."

The sheriff waited as I looked at the drawing again. He was letting me ask my questions rather than directing the conversation. "He was headed east. Blinded by the sun?"

"Sunrise that morning was at 6:17 a.m. It wouldn't have been a factor. But that also means neither was darkness. With the predawn light, he would have had good visibility."

I puzzled how he could wreck on a straight stretch of road with morning light showing his path. "Did he fall asleep?"

"We don't believe so. He navigated the curves without incident. While it's certainly possible he nodded off after the curve and then slammed on his brakes when he came back, that's doubtful in such a short period of time."

The farmer heard skidding. The police knew he'd braked hard. "Slammed on brakes?" I leaned back in my chair. "So something caused him to brake. A deer? Cow?"

"Perhaps. It certainly happens." The sheriff's fingers tapped the page repeatedly. "But that wouldn't explain the second car."

My heart raced, threatening to explode out of my chest. I had never heard about anyone else at the scene. "I thought it was a single-car wreck?"

"It was. But a second car was there."

"I thought the deputy said there wasn't another car?"

"No, I said he didn't pass another vehicle. Remember, though, he was coming back from a call. He wouldn't have seen a car going toward town."

The sheriff was holding back. I didn't know why, but he was being too careful with his answers. If he thought someone else was involved, maybe he considered me a suspect. I didn't care, though, because I needed to know. "But something makes you think there was someone else."

He held my gaze for a minute then dropped it to flip through the file folder again. He showed me a photograph of skid marks on the road.

I studied the picture but couldn't figure out what it meant. I didn't see an impact point or even tire tracks racing off the side of the road and into a tree. "I don't understand. You already said Dean braked hard."

"He did, but these aren't his marks. These were further down the road."

In front of him. Or someone passing the accident and stopping to check on him. But what did it prove? "How do you know that skid was at the same time?"

He shrugged. "We don't. They could have been down there days before."

"So why…" My frustration built. He was giving me only pieces of the puzzle. Testing me? Or giving me the news slowly? I didn't care. I wanted to know what had happened. "So there's more. What else did you find?"

That earned a grim smile as he pulled out another photograph showing tire tracks in the mud to the side of the road. Then they left mud on the road as they U-turned. "It may or may not have been who left the skid marks, but it's consistent. Whoever this was turned around and headed back in the direction of the accident site."

"But it could have been earlier?"

"Not much. It was muddy because a thunderstorm rolled through about four a.m. The road was wet, which probably contributed to Dean losing control. But that also means any mud left on the road before the storm would have washed away. So whoever turned around did it about the same time as Dean wrecked."

"But it could have been before?"

"Could have been."

He was still holding back. "But you have more."

The sheriff flipped through the photographs and pulled one out. My stomach tightened as I realized that the side of Dean's truck was in the photo. That wasn't what the sheriff wanted me to notice, though. He pointed at the ground beside the truck. "Boot prints."

Not just one but many of them. The implication horrified me. "The first responders?"

"A deputy spotted the wreck and called it in. From the time he arrived, he controlled access. It didn't take him long to realize he had a fatality, so he needed to secure the area as a crime scene. He knew what prints he left on the ground, but he took these photos to show the others." The sheriff flipped through a series of photos of the boot prints. "Notice how they come down from the pavement to where Dean's truck came to rest. Then they return to whatever car was parked there."

The next photos showed more muddy tire tracks on the pavement. "And then the car drove away. Notice in this one the approaching red light of the first volunteer firefighter on the scene and the highway patrolman just getting out of his car. The boot tracks and the tire tracks were made before anyone else arrived."

I rested my head in my hands. "So someone saw the wreck happen—"

"Or passed it after it happened."

"Turned around, stopped, walked around the wreckage, and then left without calling 911?"

"That sums it up."

"But why?"

"That's something we would really like to know. Maybe they were drunk or high and didn't want us noticing. Maybe they had something in their car they didn't want us to find. Maybe they just didn't care. Or maybe they were somehow involved."

"No clue who it was?"

"Not much to go on. Some tire tracks. Some boot prints." The sheriff propped his elbows on the table and clasped his hands together. "Which is why we talked to everyone who might have had a beef with Dean."

"Including me."

"You had a fight with Dean the night before."

"I had lots of fights with Dean."

"Exactly."

I leaned back in my chair. "So that's why you were so willing to talk to me today."

"Leaving town the day of your brother's funeral certainly looks a little suspicious, don't you think? And you were the last person to have a fight with him. A fight dozens of people witnessed."

We sat in silence, each studying the other. He was certainly testing me, trying to rattle me, but my gut told me he was looking for something else. "You don't really think I had to do anything with it."

His eyes narrowed. "And why would you say that?"

"First of all, because you didn't follow up with me."

"You left town."

"I wasn't that hard to find. My father kept a scrapbook of the towns I went to. If he could figure that out in a library, you certainly could have done it with your resources."

He stared at me then shrugged. "The deputy who interviewed you after the accident said you seemed genuinely shocked. Your mother said you were home all night." He held up his hand. "Not that you wouldn't be the first teenager to sneak out at night without your mother's knowledge. In fact, I bet I could find some people who would say you had before that night."

"So there was something else."

He sighed and pushed the photo of the boot prints at me again. "You weren't as big as your father or brother, but you did share one trait—big feet. Those boot prints are too small for you."

"You compared?"

"We compared." He folded his hands and leaned forward. "Bluntly, most victims of violent crimes know their attacker. Family is always a prime suspect. The fact that you had a fight with him put you on the radar. But nothing else made sense."

I hated to point out one important detail. "But I could have driven out there and been back before the deputy got there."

That sly smile appeared again. "The deputy who went to your house for notification checked your car. The engine was cold. The hood covered in dew. It hadn't been driven."

"You checked?"

"We checked. It's our job."

Fair enough. As much as I hated being suspected of anything, I was thankful they had been that thorough. And if they were, this meeting had a purpose.

"So why am I here now? I mean, anyone could have shown me the report."

Finally, he offered a full smile. "So the person who walked around the car could have been a stranger. It's possible. If so, we'll never find them. But I'm betting it's someone who knew Dean."

"But I wouldn't know who it was. If I did, I'd tell you. So how can I help?"

"Because whoever it was had a reason to be out on a lonely stretch of road before sunrise on a Sunday morning. And reasons usually come from something that happened recently."

"I still don't understand."

He tapped the folder with his hand. "Talk to me. What happened the night before? Tell me what isn't in the report."

21

U ntil that graduation party, the Wicked Centipedes had never played a proper show. Mostly, our music echoed off the walls of Stewart's Consignments. The shrieking fans, the crushing mobs, and the adoring crowds existed solely in our minds.

There was the senior talent show, but that didn't really count. We were only allowed five minutes, so we couldn't work through a set and take the audience on an emotional ride. They sandwiched us between a tap dancer and a baton twirler. The ends of the baton were flaming, so she won first prize.

We played three house parties, teens whose parents mistakenly thought they could be trusted in the house alone. Each time, though, the cool kids had other plans, so the celebrations were sparsely populated.

Then we had a stroke of luck. Dean, as senior class president, wanted to hold a graduation party in the gymnasium after diplomas were handed out. The principal objected, saying they had already put on a prom a few weeks earlier. Besides, there was no money.

Dean moaned about it at the dinner table. He didn't want

to do the usual drunken party at someone's house. He wanted a night everyone would remember. They couldn't do that without a good place.

After dinner, Dad loaded us up in his pickup truck and drove into town. We went into the VFW, and he showed us the hall. It had a small stage in front of an open room. As we stood there imaging the possibilities, Dad said he could rent it for us for the night after graduation.

On conditions, of course. A few of the other VFW parents of seniors would check in on the party from time to time, making sure things stayed under control. We had to clean the place after. If anything got broken, it would come out of our pockets.

Since it wasn't a school event, though, we didn't have money for anything else. No way we could hire a band or a professional DJ. Dean, Russ, and Blake compiled their music collection and stereos to make the best of it.

I had a better idea. Let the Wicked Centipedes play—no payment needed. We had assembled old speakers and amps that would be plenty loud. During our breaks, Dean and his friends would DJ using our equipment.

With the deal struck, I set about making sure it would be a night no one forgot. I figured it wasn't only going to be our first real performance. It was probably also the last. Sarah was going to college in the fall. I planned to busk all summer to make enough money to move out on my own. Xander, of course, didn't have a clue what he was going to do.

We practiced, practiced, then practiced some more. When the night came, we played our hearts out. We jumped around on stage, sweated tons, and created some awesome music. The crowd went crazy and cheered for more. We cut our breaks short, played extra songs, and did a few encores. Dean came up after, slapped me on the back, and said we were outstanding.

When it finally ended, we packed our gear with our ears

ringing and carried loads out to the parking lot. As other students swept the floors and hauled trash to the dumpsters, they kept stopping to tell us how great we were. One girl asked if we would play at her wedding. Another guy said he was planning an Independence Day party and wanted to know if we were booked yet.

Our success made me hesitate. Maybe I was being premature about skipping town. With some calls to people I knew in Asheville, we might play at some clubs down there. Maybe the Wicked Centipedes had a chance.

Xander and I walked out the door with pieces of his drum kit in our hands, our third or fourth trip to my overstuffed car. We'd crossed the dark parking lot when I spotted Dean's truck off to one side. He was leaning against it with one hand, chatting with a girl.

"Typical," Xander commented, "always making one of his smooth moves."

Buzzing with elation, I thought little of it. But as we got closer, the girl came into focus. Sarah was looking up at him and smiling, clearly enthralled with the great Dean McDougal.

What no one knew, except Sarah and I, was we were becoming a couple. We hadn't meant to date. It'd just sort of happened, but we were both worried about the impact.

We certainly didn't want to hurt Xander, whose infatuation with Sarah was obvious to both of us. He and I had formed the band, but it hadn't really become anything until Sarah joined us. After that, we rehearsed together all the time, best friends making music. Would Xander feel like a third wheel? Would it make things too awkward? If things didn't work out, would our breakup destroy the band?

Despite our resistance, though, we'd found ourselves spending time together. Talking at first. Then kissing. Then, one afternoon after school, while her father was at work, I lost my virginity in her bed.

Was it love? Lust? Or just convenience? I didn't really know, but seeing my brother—a guy who could have any girl he wanted—chatting with the only girl who had ever really paid attention to me was too much. I snapped.

Dropping my load into the parking lot, I raced toward them, screaming in rage. Dean turned too late. My shoulder hit his chest. My arms wrapped around him. I tackled him to the ground. Caught by surprise, he was defenseless. I rained punches down on him as I cursed and yelled. For a moment—a precious moment—I had the upper hand and got several licks in.

But Dean had every other advantage. He was bigger and stronger. He was athletic. He was a far better fighter. And he wasn't blind with rage.

With a twist of his body, he rolled and threw me off him. I scrambled to my feet and charged for a second time as he stood, but he blunted my assault. When I tried to connect with another swing, he grabbed my shirt with his left hand and swung hard with his right.

We had scrapped plenty of times. I guessed all siblings did. But that was the first time he really hit me. His fist caught me on the side of my face. The world blurred, and my legs went rubbery. I dropped to my knees and fell over backward. Defenseless, I waited for the next blow.

It never came.

As my eyes fluttered open, he was standing above me with an outstretched hand to help me up. I sat up and shook him off, holding the side of my head in my hands. Russ and Blake were standing by his side.

As my vision cleared, I realized to my horror that a sea of stunned faces was watching. Most of the senior class was still there helping with the cleanup and had witnessed the brawl. Russ and Blake stood with their mouths agape. Xander was off to the side, a drum still in his hands and his face pale.

I struggled to my feet and pushed Dean away. When he tried to approach me again, Russ and Blake grabbed his arms and guided him to his truck. The last time I saw him, he was behind the wheel, backing the truck out of the space. His class ring, hanging from the rearview mirror on its chain, sparkled in the reflections of an overhead light. In my daze, I thought the twinkle came from his eyes, not the jewelry. Like he was winking at me as he drove away.

As the truck peeled out of the parking lot, Sarah tried to talk to me, but I turned my back and staggered toward Xander. He asked what had started the fight, but I couldn't really tell him, because then I would have to explain about Sarah and me. Instead, I told him the truth, just not the whole truth. I'd seen Dean chatting up Sarah. We'd fought over it. Period.

When I got home, I snuck upstairs so Mom wouldn't see my swelling eye. She hated when Dean and I fought. My anger had cooled during the drive home. I didn't want to get him into trouble. Besides, I realized, I owed Dean an apology too. He didn't know how I felt, so why wouldn't he talk to her?

I checked Dean's room to see if he was there, but it was dark and empty. I guessed he had stayed over at Blake's house. He often did that when he was out partying. I decided I would apologize first thing in the morning.

Except Dean never came home.

22

The sheriff gave me directions to the accident site so I could see it for myself. Sitting in that interview room, staring at those awful photos, I'd thought that seemed like a great idea. Visit the hallowed ground. Stand on the pavement and imagine what Dean had seen on that morning before losing control of his truck. Walk the edge of the road where someone had stood at his truck and looked in on his mangled body. Like they do in the movies, maybe I would spot something the investigators had missed.

Standing outside in the parking lot under the warmth of the June sun with a copy of some of the accident folder in my hand, though, the whole notion sounded ridiculous. What could I possibly see that trained investigators had missed? After all these years, what potential evidence could exist?

Maybe, I decided, I would go later, once I'd had time to process the horrific images of the wreckage he'd shared. Until I was ready, I needed a friendly face, someone to listen to me think things through. People like that were in short supply in Millerton. Not many in my life anywhere, really.

Stewart's Consignments was a mere block-and-a-half walk.

As my sole friend in this town, Xander would be a sympathetic ear. He would help me forget those awful images.

He was leaning against the cash register in the empty store, flipping through pages of a magazine. As soon as I entered, he smiled and waved toward the back. He scooped up a pair of drumsticks from his desk and headed toward his set. "I was bouncing off the walls last night. Hadn't played in ages. It was such a blast. Could hardly sleep thinking of jamming again today." He paused when he realized I had stopped at the desk and wasn't following. "What's wrong? Is your father...?"

"He's okay. At least, he was when I left the house this morning." I stared at the wall of memorabilia above his desk. The school photos. The graduation certificate. The Camaro. The Wicked Centipedes.

The last photo drew my attention. That last performance. Eyes closed, head back, I had one hand wrapped around the neck of the guitar, the other strumming with a pick. Xander's hands were a blur as he played the drums in a drenched T-shirt. He watched Sarah at the front of the stage as she leaned forward with the microphone stand in her hand, smiling and singing. In the front row of the audience, Dean, Russ, and Blake stood at her feet, cheering.

A pang of jealousy shot through me. Sarah's eyes were locked on Dean's. She always said she sang best by picking a person out of the audience and focusing her performance on them. *Is that what led Dean to talk to her in the parking lot later that evening?*

I dropped into the chair and studied my hands. "I was at the sheriff's office looking at the accident report."

"You were in a wreck?"

Confused, I looked at him then realized he would have no reason to know what I was talking about. "Dean's wreck."

He winced. "Why would you be looking at that?"

"Coming back here has stirred up all those memories." I

pointed at the photo. "That party and playing on stage. Getting into a fight with Dean. And then waking up the next morning to find out he'd died."

"That's awful, but why torture yourself with the accident report?"

"Found out from Mom today that Dean wasn't drunk." I looked up at Xander. "I know the rest of you knew that, but I never did. I left before it came out. My parents and I... I guess we just avoided talking about it."

He tsked. "I'm really sorry. Such an unfortunate accident. These crazy mountain roads."

I stared at that photo from the graduation party. We were ridiculously happy in it, clueless our lives were about to crumble. "That's what doesn't make sense. I'd never asked exactly where it happened. I just knew he was coming home from Blake's. The spot he wrecked in wasn't curvy."

"Something else must've happened, then."

"I know." I hung my head and studied my hands in my lap. "I was headed out there to look at it but just couldn't yet. That's why I stopped by."

Xander sat down opposite me. "Then don't go. Why would anyone want to see that? You're torturing yourself for something that happened a long time ago. Sometimes, things just go wrong."

"I would, but there's more. Sheriff says someone else was there. Tire tracks show someone turned around and parked right beside the accident. Walked around the wreckage and left a bunch of footprints. And then left without calling it in."

"Oh." Xander sat back in his chair and looked toward the front of the store, though I knew the electronic chime would announce arriving customers. He'd never been good at confronting things that made him uncomfortable. Avoidance had always been his habit. It's one of the many traits we shared. Part of why we were such good friends. "Probably just the cops or firefighters, right?"

I explained to him about the deputy being the first on the scene and taking photographs right away. How the flashing red lights of the approaching fire truck were obvious in the early dawn. "So the question is whether it was someone who just got scared and left, or maybe they had something to do with the accident."

"They don't know who it was?"

"Not a clue." I leaned my head back and studied the ceiling. "That's why the sheriff had me tell him all about that night at the party. About the fight I had with Dean. Everything."

He fidgeted with a pencil on his desk. "I thought the wreck was in the morning. What does the party have to do with it?"

"They think whoever was at the accident followed him because of something that happened at the party."

"That seems like a huge leap." He stood and paced around the warehouse, running his hand through his hair like he always did when he got agitated. "Remember when we were down in Asheville and that guy tried to mug you? He had been watching you collect money in your guitar case. Maybe it was something like that."

I laughed. "Dean never had much money. Besides, no one would mug you out in the middle of nowhere."

"All I'm saying is everyone at the party loved Dean, right? You've said it yourself. Superstar."

"Well, yeah, unless he got in a fight with someone there over something."

"It wasn't that big of a building. We would've known if he had." Xander leaned forward and pointed at me. "The only person he got into a fight with that night was you."

I clasped my hands together and hung my head. "There has to be some explanation."

"There is," he said softly. "Dean had a stupid wreck. Maybe someone stopped, checked on him, and then left. It happens."

It was the most logical answer, so I nodded slowly. "I guess."

He sat down again and put his hand on my shoulder. "The accident was a long time ago. You've got enough going on with your father. It just feels like picking at this isn't healthy for you. Leave it alone."

———————

23

But I couldn't leave it alone. The accident photos haunted me too much. The twisted metal. The shattered glass. The blood-splattered seats. The same horrific scene, photograph after photograph, shot from different angles. Each shard of glass on the dash lay in the same spot. Each dried drop of blood on the seat remained affixed in the same pattern. The John Deere hat on the floorboard never shifted positions.

Nothing moved in the photos except for the graduation tassel that hung from the rearview mirror. A gentle morning breeze must have been blowing through the open doors and broken windshield. The dangling threads shifted in each photo.

Dean made me laugh at the cartoons he sketched. Caricatures of teachers, coaches, friends, and even our parents. He would magnify some physical feature, which was funny enough, but he also added speech bubbles that had them saying ridiculous things.

The best, though, were the little stickmen he drew in the margins of his textbooks. On each successive page, he would adjust the figure ever so slightly. A foot forward. A knee bent. A mouth opening into an O.

By the end of the book, the little man would have moved from one end of the page to the other, usually with a dog, a bear, or a group of other stickmen in pursuit. By flipping the pages rapidly, he could make the characters come to life, the little man racing for his life to escape his pursuers. He would fan the pages with his thumb as I giggled.

On the last days of school each year, he would spend hours erasing his art from his textbooks before turning them in. Getting grounded for defacing school property was not the way to start the summer break.

I imagined stacking the photos from the sheriff's folder and thumbing through them, making the tassel come alive, twisting and spinning in the wreckage.

I decided to do more than just visit the accident site. I retraced the entirety of Dean's last drive.

BLAKE'S CHILDHOOD home looked like almost every other house on the block. A small front yard with scraggly grass. A covered front porch the width of the house with an old couch for seating. Peeling white paint. Faded shingles.

Growing up, I had never thought of this part of town as run-down. Despite owning acres of land, we'd never considered ourselves wealthy. Money was always tight, but my parents had maintained their property the best they could. In this neighborhood, where more people rented than owned, it was different.

The mills had built these houses a century ago for the workers they'd brought in from scattered farms. The homes were functional, not luxurious, since the employees toiled long hours. By having somewhere to sleep and raise a family close by, they could work more.

When the factories closed, the corporations that owned

them sold off the houses. A few lucky employees had saved enough money to buy their own. Investors had bought others then rented them out just as the old plants had. However, the bosses no longer drove by to ensure maintenance was being done.

Anna was one of the exceptions. She owned her house, a point of pride with her. Perhaps because of that, the yard was better kept than others on the street. Or maybe Xander was just good at keeping the grass cut and the weeds pulled.

I didn't know if he still lived there. I hadn't asked. Since Anna had owned it, maybe Xander inherited it when she passed.

Sarah's old house was in between the two. Since she'd lived there for only a year, I had been inside just a few times. And mostly just to her bedroom, so I moved quickly to avoid being caught by her father or stepmother. Xander wasn't the only one we tried to hide our relationship from.

The house was laid out just like Xander's. They all probably were. A den in the front. A kitchen in the rear. A flight of steps to the second floor with two bedrooms. A slightly larger one in the back.

On that fateful morning, Blake's father had come down those steps to brew coffee and found Dean asleep on the couch. He didn't remember him coming in the night before, but he didn't remember coming home himself either. He had been hanging out at Sammy's, tossing back beers and shooting pool.

But he wasn't surprised to see Dean. He often slept there. With a swift kick to the couch, Blake's father told him to get home. Skeeter worked hard. He needed the lazy good-for-nothing home doing his chores, not sleeping the day away.

Dean grabbed a cup of coffee—much to Blake's father's dismay—and went out to his truck parked at the curb without going upstairs and saying goodbye to Blake. It was about a quarter to six when he cranked the engines. The neighbors were sure of the time because he had busted the muffler driving over a rock in a field. It woke Blake, who thought little of it before he fell back to sleep. Sarah's father heard it from his bedroom in the back of their house and cursed the noise. Plenty of people could attest to the time Dean left.

I didn't know which way his truck had faced that morning, but it didn't really matter. Whether he'd started out going north or going south, he would have worked his way out to Broad Street, the primary thoroughfare through Millerton, then turned onto the two-lane road leading to our farm, miles away.

I drove the route, thinking of my brother doing the same that morning with just the hint of the sun over the edge of the ridges to the east. Much as he would have, I slowed for the curve that caused me to lose control just a day before. Dean knew the road at least as well as I did, probably better. Up a rise, through some S-curves, down the other side—a slippery stretch of road that had seen many wrecks over the years, but Dean handled it that morning without an issue.

Then the road straightened out. A row of trees lined the right side. One of them had claimed my brother's life. On the other side of the road ran a creek, which could become a raging river during torrential rains. The water raced down the mountains and overfilled the channel, flooding the surrounding farmland at least once every few years. No houses were close to the road because of the flooding—they were all set back on the other side of the sprawling field. Because they were so far away, the residents wouldn't have heard the impact unless they were outside. Only the farmers milking their cows thought they had heard a car skidding but didn't think enough of it to investigate.

I wanted to stand where he'd taken his last breath, but I wasn't sure how to find the spot. The skid marks would have faded long ago. Would a scar still be visible on a tree all these years later? But which tree? The stretch was at least a half mile long, so I despaired. I crept down the road, searching for any sign.

Then a flash of white caught my eye. A small wooden cross nearly hidden in the tall weeds. I pulled my SUV off to the side of the road just beyond it and trudged back. The lettering had faded, but I could still make out the name.

Dean

THE ROUGH EDGES pricked my fingertips as I slid my hand along the bark of the nearby tree, feeling for imperfections. Perhaps a bump here. A divot there. Roughly the height of a truck hood.

Or maybe it existed only in my mind. Did I need to see it so badly that I could conjure it?

Stepping back, I looked at the other trees. Maybe the one he'd hit was so damaged it had been cut it down. *Should I be looking for a stump instead, the sign of another fatality from the accident?*

Of course, a backhoe could have pulled the stump from the soft mud. It wouldn't have taken too much effort.

Through the trees, I spied the background of the photos from the sheriff's department. The barn, where the farmer had been milking his cows, stood in the distance.

I returned my attention to the imperfections in the tree's trunk. This had to be it. The point of impact.

If that was true—and it had to be, just had to—then the driver's seat would have been... I paced off the distance and stood still. The low-hanging branch stretching away looked like the one I'd glimpsed through the shattered windshield in the photos, the leaves dancing in the background beyond the swaying tassels hanging from the mirror.

I was standing where Dean had taken his last breath. Or

maybe I just wanted to believe I had found the exact spot. *But if I was right, that means...*

I spun to face the road and scanned the ground between me and the asphalt. I took a step closer to the pavement and turned back to face the truck, imagining my shoes sinking into the boot prints from seventeen years earlier. Someone had stood here. Close enough to touch Dean. They could have easily helped him. But they didn't. *Who would be that callous?*

Maybe the farmer had heard the crash after all. Came out to investigate. Found Dean dead or dying. *But why not call for help? What would he have been hiding? An old still in the barn? A cash crop of marijuana hidden in the field's corner?*

But the highway patrol wouldn't have looked for that. They wouldn't have had any reason to. So it was someone else. Someone who had something to hide.

I looked down the straight two-lane road. Not a car had passed in the time I'd been standing on the side of the road. It would have been even more desolate early on a Sunday morning. Dean's headlights would have easily cut through darkness, but daylight had already been growing. The patchy fog wasn't thick enough to have fooled him into turning off the road. He knew this road as well as he knew our own fields.

Something had caused him to drive off the road. Or someone. Then they'd stood in this spot and watched him die.

I dropped to my knees and let the tears flow.

24

As emotional as I was, I wasn't ready to go back to the house and face my parents. Mom had always been able to read me, to know when I was upset. She would ask me what I'd learned from the sheriff, but I wasn't sure I wanted to tell her about visiting the accident site. But I also wasn't sure I could hide that in my current state. She had always been good at knowing when I was holding something back.

Instead, I turned around and headed back into town. Once there, though, I didn't know where to go. Everywhere held memories. Few were good.

Xander's store was out. When I'd left him, he was convinced I wasn't going to focus on Dean's wreck. He wasn't as good as Mom at figuring out what I was up to—after all, he never realized Sarah and I were dating—but I thought I was too emotional to hide from even him at the moment.

Besides, it bugged me he could dismiss the sheriff's concerns so easily. I didn't want his judgment. I wanted his support. I had always accepted his eccentricities when we were young, but that bothered me too much right now.

Still, playing music was therapeutic. Other than Xander

and Sarah, who certainly wouldn't be interested, the only other person I could get a jam session going with was Harrison. He was also the one person who hadn't known Dean or been part of my past in Millerton. Russ and Sarah may not have been wild about me talking to Harrison, but they hadn't forbidden it. And he had suggested I bring my guitar today.

I found a parking space, slung my guitar over my shoulder, and headed down the trail. If he wasn't in the meadow, then I could still play even if I was alone.

When I came around the last bend of the trail, the sounds of his music floated through the air. Relief flooded my body. I was surprised how much I was hoping he would be there. Like the day before, I crept up slowly. If he had an audience, I didn't want to intrude.

But he was alone. Back against the tree. Notebook opened beside him. Strumming his guitar. Pausing now and then to scribble a note.

I knew it well—finding somewhere to write the music that floated in my head. Getting it out was like exorcising a demon. Until I got the notes down on paper, they would bounce around my brain until I went insane.

I waited at the edge of the clearing until he looked up. "Mad Maverick. Two days in a row. And with a guitar."

I held it up by the neck. "Got it from the store that was our old rehearsal place."

"The Wicked Centipedes. My mom's told me all about the band."

"Good times."

He cocked his head. "Until you left. Mom told me that too. That you just vanished."

"I couldn't stay." I waited for him to answer, but he just stared. Maybe this had been a mistake. "I just thought we could play together. If you want to."

He leaned back against the tree and sighed. "If you answer a question."

That threw me. He acted like he was doing me a favor, not the other way around. And I wasn't so sure I wanted to be telling him things that weren't his business. He was, after all, just a kid. "Maybe. What is it?"

"Did some guy in Alabama really pull a gun on you and you took it away?"

I grimaced at the story's mythical status, told to some newspaper by a bandmate years ago and repeated by others. I had balked at telling Harrison the story a day earlier, but it seemed safe enough to just repeat what had already been printed. "Not really a big deal."

He gently placed the guitar on the ground, put his hands behind his head, and got comfortable, like a kid wanting a bedtime story. "Sounds like it was. Tell me the story."

"First, it was Mississippi, not Alabama."

THE BAND WASN'T MUCH. We were never going big. The lead singer liked girls too much, shacking up with whoever said yes on any given night. The drummer had the same problem, except with guys. And the bass player loved cocaine.

They were too interested in pursuing their vices to practice much, so our music was uneven. What we lacked in talent, we made up for in volume.

Our concert schedule consisted of fraternity and sorority houses and lots of road bars, perfect for those three to chase their demons.

Me? I needed the money. My car had died, so their communal van was my only ride. And it was my bedroom on most nights while they were off doing their deeds.

We were at some hole-in-the-wall in Mississippi. The beer

was cheap, the girls were loose, and the guys liked to fight. We got paid a cut of the door and bar receipts, so our job was to make it entertaining so people would hang out and drink.

Snake, our lead singer, had spotted his target for the night. She met all his stringent qualifications by being female and interested in him. That she was married didn't bother him in the least. We had another town to be in the next night, so we would be long gone by the time any repercussions arose.

Or so we thought.

We were doing our last set. Loud and mostly in tune. The place was hopping, and this lady was dancing around on stage with Snake while he played and sang. He even had her harmonizing with him. Well, somewhat harmonizing. Her singing was bad enough that she could have been in the band.

About that time, a big dude came busting through the crowd. He was huge. Like six feet, six inches and two hundred fifty pounds. Linebacker big. And he was livid. His face was red. His eyes were bugging out of his head. And the muscles in his arms were quivering with anger.

People on the dance floor parted like he was Moses. Well, if Moses grabbed guys and tossed them to the side as he went. His big meaty hands were just slinging dudes, and none of them were fighting back. He was too big and too mean.

He shouted, "That's my wife!"

We froze. Music stopped. The crowd fell silent. Everyone stared at this mountain of a man.

We could have gotten out of everything right then. I mean, she was just onstage dancing. It wasn't like Snake had her in bed or anything. But then she threw her arms around Snake's neck, planted a big sloppy kiss on his lips, and yelled, "Get lost, Bubba. This guy is twice the man you ever were."

I swear steam rolled out of that man's ears. He grabbed a table and slung it across the room, jumped up on stage, and whipped out a giant pistol. "He's about to be twice as dead too."

Now we could quibble that made little sense, but that was beside the point. This horse was pointing a massive gun right at poor Snake, who was frozen in fear, and squeezing the trigger.

I would have loved to be able to say I thought about what I was going to do next, but I didn't. If I had, I wouldn't have used my guitar. That thing was expensive, and I didn't have enough money to replace it. But that was the only weapon I had, so I grabbed it by the neck like I was Hank Aaron swinging for the cheap seats and crashed it down across his shoulder.

My guitar snapped right in two. Fortunately, I hit him hard enough that the gun clattered to the floor. The bad news was I didn't really hurt the guy, at least not enough to stop him. He grabbed his shoulder and focused his attention on me. I was defenseless, and my hands were now empty except for half of a broken guitar.

He took a swing at me, but I ducked under it, dove for the floor, and grabbed that pistol. I rolled across the floor, bounded to my feet, and pointed the barrel right between his eyes.

In a fair fight, he would have crushed me, but he couldn't beat a bullet, and he knew it. I held him at gunpoint just like that until the cops got there and arrested him. As they hauled him away, the crowd cheered. Then we finished our set, packed up, and got out of that town before the big guy could make bail.

———

"WHATEVER HAPPENED TO SNAKE?"

"Don't know. I quit that band less than a week later. Got

hired on by another group, a better one, and took off with them."

"And you didn't stay in touch?"

"No. Why would I?"

"Did you tell them you were leaving? Or did you just disappear on them?"

I tried to remember. I'd left a lot of bands over the years and couldn't remember the details. "Maybe I said goodbye. I don't know. It happens a lot in music."

Harrison rubbed his chin. "It's just weird you can do that so easy. Leave without saying goodbye. Never reaching out to old friends."

"Guess it's just an adult thing or something."

He twirled the pen in his hand. "Sounds stupid. I'd never do that to my friends."

"They weren't exactly my friends." He didn't look like he thought that answer was any better, so I changed the subject the only way I knew how. "So, are we going to play now?"

He thought about it for a minute then picked up his guitar. We tuned and played.

25

The house grew quiet as the sun set over the mountains. After checking on Dad, Mom and I settled into the den to watch TV. She stretched across the couch, wrapped up in a blanket, and was soon purring softly. She needed her sleep, so I shut off the TV and went upstairs. Restlessly, I flipped through the scrapbook and poked at Dean's trophies, but nothing held my interest.

With nothing else to do, I decided to sleep. When I reached to pull the covers down, I instinctively moved slowly, searching for any hidden creatures.

I had Dean to blame for this one, like most of my phobias. He was always fascinated by a wide range of critters. Spiders. Insects. Rodents. Rabbits. And yes, snakes. He'd married that with his other great hobby—tormenting me. In our yin and yang of everything, I was creeped out by all the same things he loved. That, of course, meant he'd surprised me with them as often as he could. I always worried I would find a creature in my drawers, notebook, or just dropped down the back of my shirt.

We were ten when he found the garter snake in the yard

and smuggled it into the house. While I was in the bathroom we shared getting ready for bed, he snuck into my room and slipped it into my bed. After my shower, I returned dripping wet with only a towel wrapped around my waist and whipped the cover back. Suddenly exposed to the light, the snake slithered as fast as it could for safety in the shadows of my blankets. I dropped my towel, scrambled on top of my desk, and screamed.

I wasn't proud of that.

Mom and Dad raced into the room to find me standing naked on the desk, shrieking my head off, and pointing wildly at an empty bed. Dean was doubled over in the hallway, laughing so hard he could barely breathe. Mom wore a worried face, but Dad looked like he might join Dean in the hilarity.

When they finally got me calmed down enough to explain, not to mention get me dressed, they made Dean hunt the creature down and take it outside. Then they grounded him for a week, which didn't really mean much. He still went to school, played sports, and worked around the farm, so that meant just being stuck in his room after dinner—across from me as he plotted his next chance to victimize me.

Besides, he was perpetually grounded.

After I finally felt safe enough to climb into bed and relax, I had overheard my parents talking downstairs. Dad had chuckled. "Boys will be boys."

SLEEP WAS IMPOSSIBLE, but not just because of the fear of hidden, slithering creatures. It was just past nine o'clock at night, which was very early for me. Since I was accustomed to West Coast time, where it was only six o'clock, I could only stare at the ceiling. I got dressed, left Mom a note that I would be back, and took off for a ride. The narrow, two-lane roads were dangerous enough during the day, but they were pitch-black at night. No streetlights existed this far out of town, so only the moon and stars illuminated the way.

Until I pulled into the parking lot of Sammy's Pub, I hadn't really thought about where I was going. Except for grabbing a six-pack from a convenience store, getting a beer in Miller County meant going to the Mexican restaurant out by the interstate or Sammy's, a Millerton institution for decades.

I had only peeked into the place as a teenager, though I knew Dean had snuck in a few times. They served sandwiches and burgers, so it wasn't strictly a bar and wasn't illegal for him to be there, but our parents had still forbidden it. Dean, though, enjoyed shooting pool and throwing darts, both of which he was good at, like everything else he tried. That night, I wasn't after food or games, but a beer sounded good.

When I walked in the front door, I looked around at the sparse weekday crowd. Sammy III, the current owner and grandson of the founder, stood behind the bar with a towel thrown over his shoulder. I settled onto a stool and ordered a beer. The first sip tasted cold and smooth sliding down the back of my throat.

A game of pool broke up in the back. One player came toward the bar while someone else took his place. He held up an empty mug and swayed. Shivers went up my spine in recognition. Blake Torrence.

I tried to look down, but I wasn't fast enough. Blake saw me and called out, "Freddie McDougal, is that really you?"

Trapped, I had little choice other than to nod. He stumbled around the bar and flopped down onto the stool beside me. Even in a bar, I could smell the alcohol coming off him. Sammy set a fresh mug on the bar in front of him. Blake looked at the bartender and gripped my shoulder. "You know who this is?"

When Sammy shook his head, Blake continued, "This is Dean McDougal's little brother. You remember Deano, don't ya?"

Sammy extended his hand and gripped mine in greeting. "How's Skeeter doing?"

I looked down at my glass. "Not too good."

"Sorry to hear that. He's a good man."

Blake kept his grip on my shoulder and shook me as he spoke, his words slurred. "They're all good McDougal men. Skeeter. Deano. Little Mac. Put his beer on my tab, Sammy."

"Oh yeah?" Sammy asked, his eyebrow raised. "You going to ever pay your tab?"

"Payday is coming up."

"Yeah, well, if you have too many more of those, you're going to miss work." Sammy walked away then looked back at Blake. "And you ain't driving tonight, so you better find a ride."

Blake's face turned red as he protested. "Come on, Sammy. I've only had a couple." When all he got was a grunt from the bartender, Blake turned back to me and shrugged. "Usually I can find a ride. If not, I just sleep in my truck. Done it plenty."

I didn't know what to say to him, so we sat in silence, nursing our beers. Blake swayed on his stool but managed to stay upright. Finally, he blurted, "I miss Deano. Always figured we'd hang out forever. Him. Me. Russ."

I could only agree. Not just to be polite but because it was true. The three of them seemed destined to go through life together. We managed to recount a few stories of their antics and laugh about them before the silence took over again. I turned to him. "Can I ask you something?"

"Sure." He slurred the word.

"I always thought Dean stayed that last night at your house because he was drunk."

He shook his head vigorously, wobbling on the stool. "He wasn't drunk."

"I know that now." I studied my beer. "Then why did he stay at your house? I thought he only did that when he was too drunk to come home."

"No. He almost never got drunk. He had fun without it." Blake's head turned slowly, and his eyes tried to focus on me. "Back when we were in the tenth grade, we went drinking up at the point. We all got falling-down drunk. Your mom was furious at him. Russ's parents grounded him for a month. After that, they were a lot more careful. Not saying they didn't have a beer here or there, but that's all."

That made no sense. Dean had a reputation for liking parties. Unless I had that wrong too… "If he wasn't drunk, then why'd he stay there?"

To my surprise, Blake's eyes welled with tears. He looked away quickly and took a big gulp of beer. "They did it to protect me."

"Protect you from…?" As the realization hit, I froze. "I'm sorry. I never realized."

"I told everybody at school that I got the bruises fighting. I guess that was sort of the truth. But Deano and Russ figured it out." His head drooped. His voice was so low I could barely hear him. "My old man was a good guy when he was sober…"

"But not when he was drinking," I finished for him.

Blake gripped his mug, closed his eyes, and shook his head to chase away demons only he could see. He swallowed hard and continued in a shaking voice. "When they took me home, they'd check on him. If he was drunk, one of 'em would stay. He wouldn't whale on me if they were around. And if he did, then he had to take us all on."

"So your dad was drunk that night?"

"Yeah. I'd told him before the party that Russ's dad had hired me on at the farm. Part of the pay was a trailer to live in. Dean and Russ were going to help me move out the next day after church. It made him real mad, and he sat up drinking and waiting on me to get home from that party."

He sniffled and looked around to make sure no one was close enough to overhear. He turned back and leaned toward me, close enough that our shoulders brushed, and spoke in an exaggerated whisper, "Don't tell anyone, 'kay? My old man died years ago. Ain't no reason to sully his name."

I assured him his secret was safe with me and asked him when he finally moved.

"That day. As soon as I heard about Dean. Had to. Big Mac wasn't there to protect me anymore. Not like I had much stuff, so I threw my clothes in a bag and called Russ to pick me up."

"And you lived on the farm ever since?"

He nodded. "It's great. Peaceful. Quiet. And I was never getting married anyway. Wasn't going to have kids. I read guys treat their own kids the same way they were treated. Wasn't going to put them through that. No way I'm gonna ever hit a kid."

I turned and looked at him. Really looked. Probably for the first time in my life. "You wouldn't have been the same way. You're different from your dad."

He drained his glass and held it up in the air. "I have some of the same weaknesses as him, so I'm not sure about that."

I thought about that for a minute. "You're around Russ's kids, right?"

"Not the same, Little Mac." He drew a finger in the condensation on the bar. "Russ is good with them. Sarah too. They deserve it."

I watched the men in the back throw darts. "I'm surprised they got together. Never thought of them as a couple."

Blake smiled a sad smile. "Dean probably gets credit for that too."

"How so?"

"After he died, we were all lost. And you left, so Sarah didn't really have the band to go to. The three of us spent a lot of time together, and Russ finally worked up the nerve to ask her out. It was funny because he was so nervous trying to come up with the perfect costume for their first date."

"Costume?"

"Yeah, it was a Halloween party."

Halloween? That doesn't make sense. Sarah spent much of our senior year dreaming about going to UNC Charlotte for college, back to the city where she'd grown up. Back to where her lifelong friends were. We had talked about it endlessly. I wanted to go be a rock star. She wanted to return to Charlotte. Xander... well, Xander wanted anything that wasn't his current life. I'd assumed she hadn't left because she was dating Russ. But if their first date wasn't until Halloween, why was she still in Millerton then?

Blake slumped toward the bar, his words becoming increasingly slurred. He was simply too drunk to remember what had happened seventeen years ago correctly. He wasn't going to be any more help that night.

I stood and pulled out my wallet. With a glance at Blake, I remembered Sammy's warning that he wasn't going to let him drive. I paid for both our beers and helped Blake to his feet. He swayed but managed to stay upright as I guided him to my car. He needed to go home, and I could get him there. It felt like something Dean would have done.

26

My fingers slipped over the trophies on Dean's shelf, tracing the outlines of the statuettes. A plastic boy in a crouch with the ball tucked under his arm. Another with a bat over his shoulder. One with a basketball in hand, preparing to dribble. Most valuable player. Most improved. Captain. Most points. Most tackles. All proudly displayed on those shelves.

As a kid, I would lie in bed with a book in hand as Dean sat hunched over his desk, struggling through his homework. I pretended to read, but really, I stared across the hall through his open door at those trophies taunting me with his successes.

I pretended they didn't matter to me and mocked them, calling them a bunch of cheap trinkets just to irritate him. Mostly, I had resented them. Awards didn't come to average students like me who blended into the background. Not excelling at sports or academics or much of anything.

The only awards I ever got were participation trophies, and I hated those. They screamed average. Unimportant. Not like the superstar jocks.

In my angst-filled youth, I thought that was all of him. A

jock. A dumb jock. How many times had I thought those words, not just about Dean, but his friends too?

I'd never really looked at Blake and thought of him as anything else. Never paid attention to the bruises. Or thought that maybe he hung out with his friends and played so many sports because he was scared to go home. Maybe he picked on kids smaller than him because that's all he knew.

But Dean figured it out. Every adult in Blake's life failed to protect him, but his teenaged friends found a way. No most-valuable-player trophy marked the simple act of sleeping on a friend's sofa in order to keep him safe.

What else had I missed because of my self-absorbed thoughts?

My eyes moved to the pictures on Dean's wall. A baseball team here. Football team there. Junior high wrestling team, a sport I had forgotten he'd even done. The boys stood shoulder to shoulder, serious looks on their faces.

For the first time, though, I noticed the more candid photos in frames. A celebration of a win. Teammates in a huddle. A group of boys fishing on a riverbank. Not posed but smiling faces and twinkling eyes. And Dean's arm was draped over a friend's shoulder in more than a few. He was at the center of the group, supporting them all. How many other sofas had he slept on, doing something uncomfortable because it helped someone? How often had he done that for me?

I crossed back to my room, grabbed the scrapbook off my desk, and settled onto my bed. I opened the book to the beginning then flipped slowly through the pages, really seeing them for the first time. Understanding what they meant.

Dean and I at three or four years old, playing with blocks on the den floor as sunshine flooded through the window. On that beautiful day, he could have been outside, but we were together inside. Had he stayed with me to keep me entertained after I had an allergy attack?

In a picture from a few years later—we were maybe eight

or nine years old—I was sitting in the tire swing while Dean and Russ pushed. All three of us were laughing.

A shot at the river showed Dean holding up a fish he'd caught. Russ and Blake were sitting near him with their own lines cast in the water and cheering for him. In the background, I leaned against a tree with a book in my hand, watching them from a distance.

Dad and Dean stood in the yard, working on the tractor together, both wearing overalls, with grease smeared over their faces. I sat on the front steps, watching them.

Dean, wearing a baseball uniform, leapt through the air to jump on the home plate. Russ, Blake, and others were waiting to celebrate his home run. Mom and Dad stood cheering, beaming proudly. I sat on the bleachers with my arms crossed and a scowl on my face.

Did Dean push me away? Or did I retreat? For every time he hid a snake in my bed, he'd also scooped me up and carried me home to find my inhaler. And because of a stupid accident, I'd never had the time to figure it out and tell him.

I leaned back on my bed and closed my eyes. Visions of the accident-scene photographs flickered through my mind. The twisted metal. The boot prints in the mud. The shattered windshield. The blood-splattered seats. The dangling graduation tassel.

27

"Can I ask you a question?"

Dad's eyes fluttered open and focused on me. I had found him awake when I came down for breakfast and settled into his room. We talked about the usual surface things, beating around the edges, before I plunged into the thing that had haunted my dreams through the restless night. "Was Dean easier to like?"

He snorted a laugh. I guessed the question wasn't among the ones he expected. "I loved you both. You know that."

"Not what I asked."

He closed his eyes and sighed. When he answered, I had to lean forward to hear him. "You were so different."

"I take that as a yes."

He breathed deeply. I was afraid he'd slipped back to sleep, but after a moment, he turned his head and opened his eyes again. "I was never a good student. Hated reading fancy books and never wanted to go to college. Never figured I needed it. After my father passed away, though, and I took over the farm, I saw how much I should have paid attention. Yield per acre. Crop prices. The cost of seed and fertilizer and diesel. Whether borrowing money for a new tractor made sense."

He shifted in bed and pointed to his water glass. I held it for him while he sipped from the straw. When he'd had his fill, he continued. "Dean was like me as a kid. He loved the dirt and the equipment and working outdoors, but he wanted to play through life rather than study. He was more into friends, girls, parties, and sports than he was into academics. So I figured I would teach him the business without him thinking of it as book learning. The way my daddy had done me."

"And you didn't think I needed that."

He chuckled. "Lord, no. You read more books before first grade than I have in my whole life. And then you got into music and would sit in your room scribbling in your notebooks, writing songs, and jotting down notes. It was just dots and lines to me."

I laughed at that. "Yeah, they were to me, too, at first. I could hear notes and play them back, but when a music teacher showed me a sheet of music, it seemed very weird."

He nodded. "When I was in the Army, they taught us Morse code. Your written-down music was like Morse code to me."

I'd never thought about how they were similar. "I guess they're both languages in a way."

His eyebrow rose as he thought about it. "I guess so, but different. Morse is give-me-the-facts stuff. Too hard and slow to make something magical out of it. But, in your hands, music was poetry like that Robert Frost guy we studied in high school. Or that Poe guy. I didn't understand any of that stuff or get all the meanings, but I knew it was beautiful. And hearing your music was like that. Poetry. I didn't totally get it, but I knew it was something special."

An ache built in my chest. I never knew my father to read poetry, much less appreciate it. I'd always assumed he thought it was a waste of time. I leaned forward in my chair so that we were closer. "It didn't bother you I didn't want to be a farmer?"

"Not at all." He reached out and gripped my hand with his weak fingers. "I wanted the same thing for you I wanted for Dean—to be happy."

"So you didn't resent my leaving?"

He adjusted his blankets. Ever since I could remember, I noticed he took his time answering questions. Like he was thinking of each word before he said it. "Not the leaving. Just the way you did it. Not saying your goodbyes before you took off about broke your mama's heart." He looked down at his fingers and spoke, his voice barely louder than a whisper. "And mine."

I couldn't stand seeing his eyes water, so I stared out the window instead. "I couldn't…"

But the words wouldn't come. How could I explain that I'd been so self-centered—no, self-absorbed—that I couldn't even understand how my actions would hurt others?

"I know." He shifted on the bed. "I was always trying to teach Dean that you didn't have to always be so head-on. If he wanted an answer, he asked. If he disagreed, he argued. If he had an opinion, he shouted it."

I'd always envied Dean's confidence. He could talk to anyone, stand up for himself, and have his own opinion. He didn't worry about alienating people, because everyone liked him.

Dad continued, "But you were different. You didn't try to change others' minds."

"Nice way of saying I avoided conflict." I looked down at my shoes. "It seems easier to let things be. Let people think what they want. I didn't have Dean's fearlessness. He didn't care what others thought."

"Sure he did. That's why he always wanted to deal with them straight away." He looked over at me. "He told me how he wished he had your ability to go slow. Not to be so fired up to respond so fast."

I flopped back in my chair. "He admired that?"

"Sure." Dad grinned. "He was always getting into some pickle because he leapt headfirst into some mess without thinking. Always screwing something up or making things worse because he didn't figure out the repercussions before they happened."

I snorted. "Yeah, I could always see disaster looming. Especially in his pranks and dares."

"But it wasn't always a disaster, was it?"

No, no, it wasn't. Dean could always come out on top.

He said, "You thought Dean was invincible."

I nodded, tears welling.

He sniffled. "Me too, son."

We sat in the silence for several minutes, listening to the clock in the front parlor tick and birds outside sing. After I thought he had gone to sleep, he said, "I'm sorry I wasn't better at telling you how proud of you I was."

"It's okay."

"No, son, it's not. I didn't know how to talk to you about the things you liked. I should have figured it out." He turned toward me, his eyes glassy and unfocused. "Don't be like me, son. Don't wait until you're on your deathbed to tell people what they mean to you."

I tried to speak, but nothing came out. I grabbed his hand instead and squeezed. His fingers tightened gently over mine. We stayed like that until his soft snores filled the room.

28

After pancakes for breakfast with my mother—this time without suggesting I didn't want all that food—I picked up the fallen branches under the maple tree and added them to the brush pile in the open field behind the barn. Each fall, we would burn that pile and roast marshmallows over the flames. Dad would spread the ash in the fields and till it under. "Good for the crops," he would tell us.

With the morning chores completed—and I had to smile to myself at the thought of doing chores again—I headed off to my daily jam sessions. First with Xander. Then with Harrison. Maybe I would get the three of us together before I left. Almost like a full band.

Too much of my guitar time had become about work, so it was fun to just relax and play. With those two, it was just music —not work.

When I reached the end of our driveway, though, I saw that I would be delayed. Sarah's old Ford Explorer was parked on the gravel beside the mailbox. Her arms crossed, she leaned against the hood like a sentry. She wasn't blocking my exit, but she might as well have been.

I stopped, rolled down the window, and asked innocently if she was having car trouble.

Her reply was a terse "Waiting on you." She didn't seem angry or upset, but her tone was firm.

When I got out of the car, she spied the guitar in my backseat and asked, "Are you going to the park to see Harrison?"

Instead of answering, I asked, "Do you mind?"

"Yes." She uncrossed her arms. "And no."

I hesitated. Was she rescinding her permission? "I don't know what you want me to do."

"I told you yesterday. Don't hurt him."

"And I said I wouldn't."

She looked down the road, squinting as if she saw something coming. She had something more she wanted to say, but I would have to wait for her to be ready. It had been a long time, but I still knew how she thought.

She turned back to me. "Do you have any idea how much hurt you left back here when you disappeared?"

Her tone the day before had been angry, but this was different. Unexpected. It threw me off-balance. "I thought I did. I've learned in the last two days that I hurt everyone worse than I thought."

"Your parents were devastated. They had already lost one son. And then suddenly, they had lost both."

I swallowed hard. "I know."

"And Xander. You were his lifeboat in school. He retreated into his house. He wouldn't look at me. Wouldn't talk to me. I tried. I really did."

Xander had implied she had abandoned him, but her story was more plausible.

"And me." She looked up at me with tears in her eyes. "Did you know Russ and I went down to Asheville looking for you? Asked the street musicians if they'd seen you, knew how to find you. Some of them were friends of yours. They were as shocked as we were that you left the way you did."

"I'm sor—"

She waved her hand in the air. "Harrison is waiting back at the house. He asked to borrow my car so he can drive down to the park to meet you. I just want to be clear. If you hurt Harrison the way you hurt me, I will never forgive you."

I retreated a step. "Does that mean you'll forgive me for the first time?"

"No." She turned her back and walked toward her car before slowing to a stop. Without looking at me, she said, "You haven't asked for forgiveness."

"I'm trying to right now."

She spun on her heels and tapped her foot. "I'm waiting."

"I am sorry. Please forgive me."

The foot kept tapping. "I don't think you mean it."

I looked up at the sun, squinting. Was I really sorry for leaving? Or, at least, for leaving as I did? How could I explain? "I don't think I deserve forgiveness."

Her foot stopped, and her face softened slightly. Not much. She needed more. I owed her more.

"When I left, I thought I knew everything. That my father didn't care about me." I told her about finding the scrapbook and the conversation I'd just had with Dad.

"What else?"

I hung my head. "I always thought of Blake as an entitled jerk. I never wondered why. Then I find out Dean knew what he was going through. Russ knew. Last night was the first conversation I ever really had with him."

"He told us all about it this morning." When I raised an eyebrow in surprise, she continued. "He was worried he said something he shouldn't have."

"About what his father did?"

She shook her head. "He doesn't usually talk much about

that, but he's mostly come to terms with it. As well as anybody ever does, I guess."

"Then what?"

She didn't help me, so I puzzled through the conversation. The only other thing that stuck in my mind was his comment about when she and Russ started dating, but why would she care that I knew that? "Was it the Halloween thing?"

She wrung her hands and looked back over her shoulder before nodding at me.

"Yeah, I wondered why you were still here. I mean, I thought you were going to college."

"Well, I didn't."

"But why not?"

"You can be so dense sometimes." She grunted in exasperation. "Remember I told you Harrison got his driver's license this spring?"

My mind raced, trying to piece that information together. Halloween. Driver's license. Sixteenth birthday. In the spring. March. *Which means…*

As realization sank in, the sounds of the birds faded, daylight dimmed, and the muscles of my body froze. My voice sounded far away as I finally asked, "Harrison isn't Russ's son, is he?"

Her arms dropped to her sides. She tilted her head back to look into the sky and loosed a long, slow, nervous breath. "Nope."

I paused. Fear knotted my stomach as understanding began to sink in, but I couldn't say it aloud yet. "Does Russ know?"

She laughed, not a funny laugh but a disgusted one. More a huff than humor. "Of course. He knew when he asked me out for Halloween."

I fidgeted, wanting to ask the obvious. Harrison knowing who I was had nothing to do with my musical talent. Sarah and I had dated only briefly, only a few weeks. But the truth was we hadn't really dated, because I didn't want Xander finding out. Dating had meant sleeping together.

Finally, I blurted out, "Is he mine?"

She shook her head in disgust. "You're an asshole if you have to ask."

My stomach flopped. I was still resisting the possibility. "Well, I mean, you, Dean…"

"Yep, still an asshole." She glared at me. "Dean asked me out. I said no. Because I was dating you and I thought that meant something. It did to me. To Dean too. Just not to you."

"I'm—"

"Don't say you're sorry. Not until you really mean it." She avoided my eyes by looking down the road. "Do you know Dean came by later and apologized?"

That caught me off guard. *When did he have time to see her after the graduation party?* "Later that night?"

"The next morning. I was sitting on my front porch like I did every morning, reading a book. He was leaving Blake's and saw me as he was getting into his truck. He came over to say he didn't know you and I were dating. Congratulated me. Gave me a big hug. We chatted for a bit before he left."

"That means…"

"That I was the last person to talk to Dean. Yes."

"The sheriff thinks Blake's father was the last person."

She shrugged. "I didn't see how it mattered to the cops."

It probably didn't, but something nagged at me. "I wish I had known."

"I tried to tell you. Called and left messages. Came by your house, but you wouldn't see me. I tried to catch you at the funeral."

"You're right. I was an asshole."

"Still are."

I couldn't argue with that as my mind reeled with so many

things I hadn't known. *What else do I have wrong?* "Did you know then?"

"That I was pregnant?"

I nodded.

"No. I didn't find out until later that summer. Would it have made a difference?"

Great question. Would self-centered, eighteen-year-old me have stuck around if he'd known? Or would I have run even faster? As much as I didn't want to admit it, I knew what I would've done. It took everything I had for thirty-five-year-old me not to race away. "I am truly sorry."

She tilted her head and looked at me. "That one, I finally believe."

I stood there with my hands shoved in my pockets, unsure what to do or say. I had a son. Or, more accurately, I had fathered a child. I barely knew him. "How should I handle it?"

"I only have one request. Don't you dare lead Harrison on. If you're going to leave, be man enough to tell him goodbye to his face. If you can't promise me that, leave him be while you're here."

I agreed. "So he knows?"

"Yes. He's known for a few years. He deserved to, so we told him when we thought he was old enough to understand."

"How did he handle it?"

"About as well as you think. Angry. Hurt. Confused." She looked across the road at their driveway entrance. "But, over time, he came to understand. Accept."

He was more mature than I'd been at his age. Honestly, more mature than I was now. But it did explain his terseness when talking to me. He was chatting with the man who had abandoned him, even if I didn't know. "What about my parents?"

Sarah cast her eyes down. "We never told them. You know

how small towns can be about such things. We discussed it with Harrison, and we agreed to keep it among ourselves for now."

My parents had a grandson and didn't know it. I couldn't imagine how much that might mean to them.

Sarah continued, "Harrison has made a point of being over at your house so he could get to know them, but he wasn't ready to tell them. Now, with you in town, he thinks it would be okay. He asked for permission last night."

The reason for our chat became clear. It wasn't really about me. "But to tell them, you had to tell me." I thought for a minute. "Does Harrison know you're talking to me?"

"He wanted to tell you. We talked about how to do it last night. I told him I would let you know before you saw him today." She locked eyes with me. "I warned him you might not show up once you found out."

"So you're telling me for him, not for you?"

She nodded.

"So you really don't want me to talk to him, but he does?"

She put her hand on her car door handle. "I trust my son. I don't trust you. Don't hurt him."

29

When I arrived at Xander's store, he was once again sitting on the stool behind the cash register, this time working a crossword puzzle in a folded newspaper. He sat it down on the counter, crossed his arms, and studied me. "You went out there anyway, didn't you?"

I stood with the guitar in my hand. Unlike the day before, I didn't want to talk so much as play music. I was tired of talking. "Is that so bad?"

He waited a few seconds then sighed. "I'm just worried about you. That's all. You're acting like the accident was last week, not nearly two decades ago."

"For me, in a way, it was last week. I thought I knew what happened. Now I realize I don't. And that opened everything back up for me."

He pursed his lips in thought. "I guess I get it. I never had a brother or sister, so it's like you're the closest thing to it I ever had. If something happened to you…"

I wanted to explain how I needed to know, how much I'd learned about my brother since coming back to Millerton. At the same time, I was tired of talking about it at all. Instead, I pointed toward the storage area with my guitar. "Are we going to play or what?"

He shrugged, got up from the stool, and walked through the curtain. Seeing the pictures on the wall, I paused again and let my eyes slide over them. The school photos. The diploma. The Wicked Centipedes. The three of us sitting on Sarah's front porch.

In the corner of that last photo was Anna's prized Camaro. I pointed at it. "Whatever happened to your mom's car?"

He turned and looked at it. "I still have it."

"That's cool." I studied the photo. "We used to beg her so much to let us drive it."

A sad smile stretched across his face. "I understand better now why she resisted letting us take it out. I'm always having to work on it to keep it running smoothly. Can barely afford the parts and certainly can't pay for a mechanic as much as she needs it."

"Don't I know it. When my old clunker wouldn't start, I wished I had paid more attention to guys like you and Dean and my dad about how to fix things."

He shrugged. "Best class in high school was auto mechanics. I could actually pass those exams."

I ran my fingers lightly over the photo. The car twinkled in the sunlight, probably because Xander had washed and waxed it. In the years since, I'd forgotten how much attention he paid to it. It made sense he would have kept it after his mother passed.

"You still live in your old house?"

He shook his head. "Made no sense keeping it with just me. I don't know how Mom scraped up enough for the mortgage and repairs. I can barely afford the rent for the dump I'm in. So I sold it, paid off the loan, and used what was left over to keep this place afloat."

My finger followed the lines in the photo back to Sarah's

porch, where the three of us sat on the steps, laughing. "Did you know Dean visited her that last morning?"

For a minute, Xander didn't respond. Finally, he said, "How do you know he did?"

"Sarah told me this morning. The two of them talked before he left Blake's house."

"Why?"

"He apologized to her for chatting her up the night before. For asking her out."

"Why would Dean apologize for asking her out?"

"He didn't know we were dating."

Xander dropped his drumstick.

I turned to see him standing there with his mouth open.

"Dating? You two?"

Keeping our relationship from him seemed like the silliest thing ever in the light of adulthood. Sure, it might have caused a rift between us, but we would have figured it out. We always did. "Sorry. It was stupid, but we never said anything because we didn't want to hurt you."

"Wow. I didn't…" He bent over and picked up the stick. When he straightened back up, he asked, "For how long?"

"Just for a few weeks. We kinda fell into it. Were just talking one night, and next thing I knew, we were making out. I was trying to figure out how to tell you and then Dean's accident and me leaving. I guess we just never talked about it."

"That means…" He twirled the stick in his hand and paced back and forth. "So they never dated?"

"Who?"

"Dean."

"Oh. No. Like I said, when he found out, he apologized to Sarah. He probably would have apologized to me to, but…" *But he was dead.* That one was hard to say.

"But then…" He paced some more. "Harrison? He's yours?"

What have I done? Not thirty minutes earlier, I'd promised Sarah I wouldn't hurt Harrison, but here was Xander, asking about something they didn't talk about in town. "Please. You can't say anything."

"Wait." He held up his hand, absent-mindedly twirling the drumstick in his hand as he thought. "You left your pregnant girlfriend and ran?"

"No, it wasn't like that. I mean, yeah, it was, but I didn't mean to." I took a deep breath and tried again. "I didn't know she was pregnant. She didn't either. It was too early."

The stick kept twirling. "When did you find out?"

"This morning. She just told me."

He sat down heavily in the desk chair. "I thought he was Dean's."

Despite Sarah's accusation, apparently I wasn't the only asshole who'd wondered that. "You didn't think Russ was the dad?"

He snorted. "No one in town believes that. She was already showing when she and Russ started dating. Rumors went wild about who the daddy was, but the bet was Dean."

Confusion swirled through my brain. "Why Dean, though? I mean, I get why I thought so, but…"

"The fight. Everyone saw it. Or at least, a lot of people did, and they talked about it, so everyone knew it. So that meant everyone knew Dean was talking to Sarah. It wasn't rocket science."

"But no one thought of me?"

Xander cackled. "Hell, I was your best friend, and I never suspected you. Why would anyone think you were in Sarah's league?"

Ouch. But sadly understandable. "Then what did everyone think the fight was about?"

He shrugged. "Because I knew you had a crush on her too.

We talked about it all the time. I figured you were protecting our friend. I just didn't know you had... you know..."

I looked at the photo of that last concert. Him staring at her. Her looking at Dean. "Xander, I—"

He cut me off with a wave of his hand. "It was a long time ago, okay? If I'd known, I don't know how I would have reacted. But today—now—it doesn't really matter anymore, does it?"

We sat together, our thoughts floating into the past, while I held my guitar. Finally, I asked, "So, do you want to play?"

He fingered the sticks on his desk and glanced back at the drum set in the corner. "Just give me a little time to process everything, okay? Maybe tomorrow."

I stood and studied his wall of mementos again. We looked so happy in that last photograph. *How did it go so wrong?*

I left with the guitar in my hand.

30

As I approached the clearing in the park with my guitar, fear bubbled inside my gut. I was still struggling to come to terms with the bombshell Sarah had dropped on me that morning. Not that I didn't deserve to suffer.

Would Harrison even be in the clearing? Now that he knew I knew, he would probably be furious. Our conversations had been tense already, and now I understood why. With things out in the open, I wasn't sure he would want anything to do with me at all.

Every fiber of my body screamed to run back to my car. Drive away. Avoid. My fight-or-flight response had always chosen flight. I'd run from every bad situation in my life.

I took a deep breath. Not this time. I'd promised Sarah I wouldn't leave without saying goodbye to Harrison. If he never wanted to see me again, I would honor that. I would at least, though, look him in the eye before I left. I owed him that much.

The closer I got to the end of the trail, the more convinced I became that the meadow would be empty. I even half hoped it. No music floated up the path. No guitar strummed. No voice sang a chorus. I heard only birds chirping in the trees.

But when I rounded the bend, I saw him leaning against the trunk of the tree with his guitar lying on the ground beside him. He waited until I was nearly to him before he spoke. "I wasn't sure you would show."

I stood, holding my guitar. "I wasn't sure you wanted me to."

"Neither am I." He studied me for a moment. "Well, are you going to sit or not?"

On my walk down the trail, I had debated what to say when I saw him. *How do you start a conversation with a son you never knew you had?* I wasn't good at conversation without pressure. And I avoided it totally when the pressure was there. I started out clumsily after I settled into a sitting position. "I'm trying to wrap my head around this dad thing."

He held up a hand to stop me. "I have a dad. A great one."

"Fair enough. You're lucky. Russ is far better at that than I ever would be." I ran my hand along my guitar strings. "Maybe I'm just a guy you can talk to about music."

He shrugged, clearly unimpressed with my answer. "I've got music friends too."

I knew what he was doing because it was exactly what I had done a thousand times before. When things got uncomfortable between me and someone else, I pushed them away. Shut them off.

What he wanted was for me to leave. Except I wasn't going to. Not this time. I'd been walking away my whole life. From Millerton. From bands. From friends. From my own family. All it ever got me was away, living in a dump of an apartment that I could get evicted from if I didn't find a way to make some money. And that was tough because no band wanted to hire me—they thought I would just quit on them too.

He could get up and leave. I wouldn't chase him if he did.

But I would not turn first. Let him test me. He deserved that much. "So, what do you want from me?"

He leaned back against the tree, his face scrunched in thought. "I've listened to Mom and Dad's stories about you. Seen you on videos online. But it feels like I've got nothing. It's like you're not real. Tell me something, anything, about you. Something no one knows. Give me something to figure out if you're worth the time."

That was a tough one, so I told him the only thing that came to mind.

THE BAND I was playing with that night in Mississippi really was bad. The lead singer liked women too much, the drummer chased men, and the bass player snorted too much cocaine. All of that was true. Not much else was.

The crowd was sparse. Maybe thirty or forty people. Mostly falling-down drunk dudes out for a night on the town with their girlfriends. They didn't know who we were, and they didn't care.

Snake was eyeing this lady drinking alone, and he started chatting her up during breaks. She was ten to fifteen years older than him and at least fifty pounds heavier. But Snake, being Snake, didn't care. Our cut of the door would not be much, barely enough to cover gas to the next town on our schedule, but he could use his free drinks to get her drunk. Somebody dropped a dime on him, though. Called her old man and told him what was going on.

We were playing our last set. That woman was on stage, stumbling around drunk and warbling into the mic. Next thing we knew, some guy was shouting at us.

He was big. Not muscular, but fat. Huge. Three hundred fifty pounds at least. And stumbling drunk. Weaving from table to table. Knocking over chairs. Pushing people out of the way. The whole time, he's yelling, "That's my wife!"

Snake was eyeing the woman, trying to decide if she was worth the trouble. The bassist was already easing his way off the stage. The big guy grabbed a full pitcher of beer and slung it at Snake, but he was too drunk to throw straight. It came flying directly at me, soaked my clothes and guitar, and dripped on my amp.

I could barely afford to eat, let alone buy a new amp. All I wanted to do was dry my equipment before it shorted out. So I moved forward. The big dude climbed onto the stage and hit a microphone stand. The stand came down right in my path, and I fell over it. So there I was, all of one hundred fifty pounds, soaking wet—which I was, in beer—and I collided into a wall of blubber more than twice my weight. The only thing going for me was that he was drunk, so he fell backward. In his panic, he reached out for anything to grab, which turned out to be the guitar strapped around my neck.

I tried to stay upright, but it was impossible. No way I could resist all that weight. The strap or my back was going to break, or I was going to fall.

I fell. We crashed off the stage and slammed into the floor. He landed on his back. That knocked the wind out of him. I landed on top of him. He probably didn't even notice scrawny little me as I bounced off him like he was a trampoline. My poor guitar, unfortunately, was between us. I crushed it in the fall.

When we slammed to the floor, a gun he had tucked into his waistband came loose and clattered across the floor. In about the only lucky thing that happened that night, I bounced off his gut and landed on top of the gun.

I didn't wrestle it from him. I didn't even think about what it meant. I just stood up with it in my hand. And that was when panic set in. He was on the ground. The gun was in my hand.

My guitar was shattered. I could barely catch my breath. I couldn't even think straight enough to figure out if I'd shot him and didn't remember it. I almost pissed my pants in fright.

A bunch of good old boys grabbed me and took the gun away. Another group held him down. Next thing I knew, cops were coming through the door, and everyone was saying I pulled a gun on this guy. Nobody had seen which one of us had it at the beginning. Even if they had, they probably wouldn't have been on the side of some skinny, long-haired musician from out of town.

I tried to explain what had happened, but they hauled me down to the jail because they didn't believe me. The next morning, though, they let me know the guy was telling them it was his gun, not mine. He wasn't doing it to protect me. He just wanted his gun back.

Anyway, the serial numbers proved it was his.

He, of course, said he'd never pulled it out or anything, which was true, so I must've taken it from him during the fight. Now, there wasn't a fight, but all I wanted was out of town. The guy said he didn't want to press charges, and I sure didn't, so everything got settled without any fuss. The cops wrote it up just like he told them. They warned me never to come back to town, like I had any plans to do that.

I caught back up with the band, and we skedaddled. The whole drive to the next town, Snake complained he'd never gotten laid.

Next thing I knew, someone in the band told the story to a newspaper. Probably Snake, though I never found out for sure. He must've thought it would make the band sound tougher.

A reporter pulled the police report, which said I had taken the guy's gun from him during the fight, and shared the story. The band started calling me Mad Maverick McDougal.

I was going to tell the truth, clear up the whole mess, and stop the stupid lie, but I got a call from another band who had heard the story and offered me a job. I wanted out of that awful band I was in, so I took it. Then I couldn't tell them the truth because it was the whole reason I'd gotten the gig.

So that's the whole sordid story.

HARRISON LEANED against the tree while I waited for his reaction. "So you let everyone believe a lie for a job?"

I thought about that for a moment. I'd never told anyone the truth about what happened that night. "Not for the job. Yeah, at first, maybe, but also because it was easier than admitting the truth." I paused for a minute and realized there was more to it. "But it was the way people looked at me too. For the first time in my life, they didn't see some scared punk who let people run over him. They saw a guy who stood his ground against a man twice his size. An armed man."

"But you didn't."

"No," I admitted. "I haven't done it much in my whole life. But it felt good that people thought I could."

He chewed on his lip as he thought that over. Finally, he nodded. "That makes sense."

It did because it was the truth, not something I told myself much. But saying it aloud made me realize something more. "You know what I really want?"

"What?"

"To know for myself that I can stand my ground. I don't want it to be a lie. I want it to be real."

Harrison stroked his guitar in thought for a few minutes. Finally, he looked up at me and cocked his head. "Mom says you used to busk the streets in Asheville."

I nodded.

"That took guts, didn't it? Playing your guitar in front of strangers. No stage. No separation. Just you and them."

"Yeah, I guess it did, but I think music made it easier."

He picked up his guitar and strummed a few chords, tuning as he went. "Maybe. But it still takes guts."

I'd forgotten about my nervousness that first time Anna and Charlie got me to play in Asheville. I never would have done that without them conspiring to make it happen. I'd wanted to run away so badly. But I'd stood there. And played. Conquered my fear. And that had felt good.

I looked Harrison in the eye. "I'll do whatever you want. Leave if you ask, but I'll be blunt. I'd prefer to stick around. Get to know you some." I paused, waiting for a reaction. When I didn't get one, I said, "If that's cool."

He fingered his guitar as he thought. He didn't say yes. But he didn't say no either. "Let's play a few songs."

We played more than a few as the afternoon passed.

31

W hen I returned home, I checked in on Dad. He slept fitfully, murmuring in his sleep. Mom sat in the chair in the corner, a book in her lap, eyes closed and snoring softly.

I wanted her to get her rest while I prepared our dinner, which was little more than selecting one of the many casseroles from the refrigerator and sliding it into the oven. The noise, though, woke her. She joined me in the kitchen and chopped fresh vegetables for a salad then shucked corn.

While we worked together in the kitchen, I wanted to tell her about Harrison. He was, after all, her only grandson. My leaving, no matter what might have happened between Sarah and me, had deprived her of watching him grow up as one of her own. She would recover from any shock with the joy of being a grandmother.

I held back, though. What little relationship I had with Harrison was too fragile. To build trust, I needed to plan each step with him—and his parents. Small towns loved their gossip. This would be seismic news.

After eating our early supper, we sat rocking on the front porch. We didn't need to talk to enjoy each other's company. A vehicle coming up our gravel driveway broke our quiet. My gut tightened as Russ Caldwell's pickup truck came into view, followed by a cloud of dust. He parked beside my rental and approached the porch.

Other than our brief exchange in the park, we hadn't spoken since my return. Had I said or done something earlier in the day to upset Harrison? Perhaps Sarah had revoked her permission for me to talk to the boy. Or maybe Russ had his own opinion and was going to forbid me from any further contact.

I held my breath as he exchanged pleasantries with Mom, asking about Dad and her day. Then he asked her, "May I borrow Freddie for a few minutes?"

We left her rocking on the porch as we walked across the yard and entered the barn. Without having to search for the switches, he flipped on the lights and walked deeper into the gloom. He came to a stop at one of the thick supports and ran his hand along the rough-hewn edge. He paced, checking other signs of disrepair even my out-of-practice eyes noticed. A hook dangling on a broken nail. A rusted pulley. Frayed ropes. "I'm planning to fix this building up come winter. Patch a few leaks. Replace some rotting boards."

"You need the storage?"

He leaned his back against the post. His shoulders bunched in an almost-imperceptible shrug. Russ had taken on the stoic characteristics I remembered of his father. "Not yet. Have to keep up on the maintenance, though."

How many times had I heard my father say those words? "Have to take care of the things you own, son, so they'll last," he would say. And that was what Russ was doing. He owned these things now.

I asked, "The house too?"

His head moved in the slightest of nods. "Yep."

"Because one of your kids will move into it someday?"

He shifted. "Don't worry. I keep my promises. Libby lives in that house for as long as she wants. I'm in no rush. The kids are years away from needing their own place."

"Harrison is sixteen."

The edges of his mouth turned up. "I'm talking Brandon or Brenda. Maybe both. Harrison won't stay in Millerton."

"Because of music?"

"Because he's not a farmer."

"And that's a bad thing?"

Russ tilted his head and eyed me. "Is that what you think?"

Uncomfortable under his stare, I walked into a shadowy corner, inspected a hay bale for a hidden snake or mouse, then sat on it. "No, of course not. I left, didn't I?"

"Not that." He looked up at the ceiling in thought. "You believe Skeeter thinks less of you because you didn't want to be a farmer?"

I picked at the straw in the bale. "Used to think that way, but I'm starting to see Dad understood me more than I realized. Things were certainly easier for Dean because he didn't want to leave."

Russ chuckled. "Are you kidding? Dean and I spent hours talking about ways out of Millerton. Military. Go to the community college and learn a trade. Just disappear, like you ended up doing."

That stopped me cold. I couldn't imagine either of them somewhere else. "Why didn't you leave?"

He crossed the dirt floor and sat beside me. He didn't bother checking for varmints first. "When I was seventeen, my dad woke me one night about two in the morning. I had school the next day and some big test, but he needed my help, so I got dressed and followed him. A cow was calving and was in distress. We were going to lose both of them if we didn't help. A few hours later, covered in mud, blood, and shit, I was sitting on my tired butt, watching that calf take its first step while its mom nuzzled it. I was freezing cold and knew for sure I was going to fail the test. But instead of hating it, I realized I couldn't be happier."

I snorted. "Sounds awful to me."

"Of course it does. It's why you needed to go out into the world. Skeeter knew that. I knew it. Dean knew it."

I stared at my hands in my lap. "I thought Dean hated me for it."

Russ squeezed my shoulder, his calloused hands digging into my skin. "Dean envied you for it. He never stopped wanting to leave and was so jealous you were actually doing it."

"But…" I struggled to understand my brother envying me for anything. "Didn't he have a moment like you did? Wanting to be a farmer?"

He shook his head. "Don't get me wrong. He hadn't decided he *didn't* want to be, but he hadn't decided he did either. He just didn't think he had a choice."

"Sure he did. Just like I did."

Russ clasped his hands together and looked away from me. His voice was quiet in the hush of the barn. "Dean understood you would never be happy here. Going out into the world and making your music was your only choice. But that meant Skeeter had nobody to take over the family farm if Dean left. He was the last McDougal. Two hundred and fifty years weighed on his shoulders. Hobard McDougal sending his demands from the grave. Other than you, nobody defied the McDougal legacy. He was scared to tell Skeeter he wanted to leave too."

Trying to imagine Dean scared of anything or anyone was nigh impossible, but picturing him fearing Dad was even harder. They talked about everything. Or at least, so I'd thought.

Besides, I couldn't imagine Dean being anything but a

farmer. He loved the dirt and the sweat. "What did he want to do?"

Russ smiled. "Depended on the day. Motocross racer. Firefighter in some big city. Marine. Forest ranger. Pirate on the high seas if he could figure out a way. Something outdoors, physical, adventurous."

"He never told Dad?"

"Didn't think he could. And once he died, I told no one until now. No point in that." Russ stood and ran his hand along the rusted pulley. "But that's why I'm so careful to let Harrison know he can do what he wants. Brandon and Brenda too."

"And if none of them want to stay in the business?"

"Then when I'm too old to do it, I'll sell the place. Sarah and I will go live on a beach somewhere."

I laughed. "I can't see you living on a beach."

That earned a smile from him. "Fine, a cabin deep in the woods. It doesn't matter to me. Though I think Sarah would pick the beach, and I'll do whatever she wants."

In my self-centered youth, I'd never really paid attention to the type of person Russ was. A guy who would go on a sleepless night to save the lives of cattle. Who would make sure his kids did what they wanted with their lives. Who would live anywhere just because his wife wanted to. I could see how Sarah had fallen in love with him.

As I watched his hand on that pulley, I noticed what wasn't there. "You don't wear a wedding band?"

"Too dangerous to wear during the day. Get it caught in machinery and rip a hand off. Or lose the thing out in some field." He spread his fingers and looked at them. "It's in a box in our bedroom. Every night when I go home, I take a shower and put it on. It's just a simple gold band. I'm not much of a jewelry guy."

I thought of some of the musicians I'd played with. Necklaces. Rings on fingers, noses, ears, and other places not worth mentioning or imagining. Realizing how not dangerous our work was compared to Russ's made me smile. "So, the wedding band is the only jewelry you own?"

He pursed his lips in thought. "That and my old class ring, but I only take that thing out once a year for the homecoming game. Stays in the box the rest of the year." He shrugged. "Seemed like a big deal to have one back in the day, but not so much now."

I looked at my own ringless fingers. Over the years, I'd owned many rings to flash on stage. I had pawned them all in the last few years since the work dried up. "I remember Dean saving every penny he could to get one."

"I probably should have saved my money. Those things were expensive."

Thanks to my busking cash, I could have afforded to buy one more than anyone else, but I never saw the point. But for guys like Dean and Russ, they mattered more. Maybe it was school pride. Or maybe it just was the way people were wired. When Dean got his, he wore it everywhere. "I could help Harrison buy his."

Russ turned back to me and smiled. "Feel free to offer, but I think he'll pass. He has shown no interest."

"So you're okay with me talking to Harrison?"

His face grew serious, and he locked eyes with me. "Sarah said she told you she would hunt you down if you hurt him?"

I nodded.

"I'll be right beside her."

I swallowed hard.

He continued, "But as long as we're clear on that, yes, I'm okay. In fact, I think it's a good thing."

Tension I didn't realize I was holding drained from my body. Russ's acceptance surprised me. "You'd do that for me?"

"Not you. For Harrison." He picked at his fingernails and spoke softly. "I mean no disrespect to your father, but I watched

Skeeter with you. He tried to do the right thing by you but couldn't figure out how. I'm no smarter than him—learned the half of farming my father didn't teach me from him—but I don't want to make the same mistakes. The truth is, I don't know music and don't understand it. Sarah does, of course, but he needs to know I support him. Letting him learn from others, especially from you, is the best way I know how."

He turned to me. "So I'm not giving permission. I'm asking for your help. Can you do that for me?"

My mind spun, and I sputtered, "What if he decides music isn't for him?"

"That's fine too. All I care about is he's happy."

As we shut off the lights and walked back to the house, I admitted to myself for the first time that maybe I wasn't leaving quickly.

32

Before Russ left, we discussed telling my parents about Harrison. We both thought it was the right thing to do, but we also wanted to ensure we moved at a speed Harrison was comfortable with. The repercussions would affect him more than any of us. Russ committed to discussing it with Sarah and Harrison that evening.

As he drove away, a tightness spread through my chest. Guilt seeped through my body.

My whole life, I'd run from conflict. Was that the real reason I so readily agreed to delay telling my parents about Harrison? Maybe I wanted to avoid seeing the hurt and confusion on my parents' faces. That's why I left Millerton without telling anyone goodbye. No one was going to stop me. No matter how much I tried to justify it in my mind, I just didn't want to have to deal with their feelings.

I stuffed my hands into my pockets and walked through the rows of corn, deep in thought. This felt different than running and avoiding. I wasn't deciding based on how it affected me. This was about Harrison. For the first time in a very long time —possibly ever—I was acting based on someone else's needs. I didn't want to avoid things just because it was easier. One more day, I promised myself. Unless Harrison wanted more time.

As the last of the day's light faded from the sky, I made my way back to the house and inside. Knowing I was doing the right thing didn't make it any easier to face Mom. She didn't ask what Russ and I had discussed.

Fortunately, it didn't take long for Mom to settle on the couch for the night. I sat in a chair near her feet and talked, but within a few minutes, her soft snores stopped me. I adjusted the blanket covering her and turned off all the lights except for a single lamp, enough for her to see in case Dad needed her.

Before going to bed, I settled into the chair in his room. His chest rose and fell as he wheezed, but he never woke. As the hour grew later, the world outside fell silent except for the lone owl hooting from the barn.

I stood to retreat upstairs but paused when I reached the doorway. I turned back to look at him, the light from the next room casting a soft glow on his face. I had grown to understand him better in the past few days. How he cared for me even if he struggled to show it. How I'd hurt him even if I'd never meant to.

I crossed the room and gently brushed his thinning hair. Then I leaned over and kissed his forehead. Tears blurred my vision as I left his room and climbed the steps.

As had become my habit, I turned on a lamp in Dean's room and sat on his bed, staring at his trophies. I wondered how often he had lain here dreaming of leaving Millerton. I wished I had realized he wondered about his possible futures like I did. We could have shared our dreams.

The more I learned about him now, the more I realized I hadn't understood him when we were kids. I'd lived just across the hall and not known my own brother as well as his friends had. Maybe we'd always been destined to be two strangers growing up under the same roof.

Maybe he'd understood we were drifting apart. Had he been trying to get my attention by putting a snake in my bed? Or by showing off his knowledge of the family? Or even coming to my defense when a group of bullies took my lunch money?

For all the times he'd had my back, let me hang out with his cooler friends, or even just pushed me in a tire swing, I hadn't shown the least bit of gratitude. He had always been there for me, and I had never given him a simple thanks.

With a disgusted grunt at myself for wallowing in doubts, I pushed myself to my feet. Rather than crossing the hall to my room, though, I studied the photos on his wall. At the one of me in the tire swing, Russ and Dean laughing and pushing, I paused and ran my finger over the frame. I ached to remember how things were back then, what the air smelled like, how the wind felt across our faces.

Restless, I opened the desk drawer and flipped through the contents. Pencils. Pens. Paper clips. Rubber bands. A few old coins. I stood in his closet and stroked his high school letter jacket and the denim coat beside it. I leaned forward and sniffed the denim. Did it still contain a hint of his sweat? Or was that just my imagination? Did I even remember what he smelled like?

Slipping on that lined denim jacket, I realized the shoulders were too broad and the sleeves too long. Even all these years later, Dean's hand-me-downs were too big for me. I couldn't bear to take it off, though, despite the fact it was too much coat for even a cool mountain evening.

From the chest of drawers, I retrieved the small cardboard box. Flipping through it again, I handled the high school graduation tassel, the one I had seen hanging from his rearview mirror in the accident photos. I toyed with the key ring with a rabbit's foot and keys to his truck and the house. I picked up the old wallet and extracted his driver's license, a library card, school ID, and the seventeen dollars in cash. Through my teary eyes, I could barely read the truck's registration and insurance card contained in an envelope. When I picked up the old white choker he used to wear around his neck, I couldn't hold back any longer and let the tears flow.

The box, I realized with some horror, contained things recovered from the accident scene or out of the pockets of the clothes he had been wearing that morning. From the reports, I knew the police had carefully inventoried everything. Now I knew they had returned it all, even the seventeen dollars.

And my parents, in their grief or out of practicality, hadn't buried the white choker with him. Or removed the cash. Or even trashed that ratty old rabbit's foot. They had kept everything he had with him that day. Had they stood here like I was, fingering inconsequential trinkets while thinking of Dean?

The more I flipped through the box, the more I felt something was off. What didn't belong? In a flash, I realized I had it backward. What bothered me wasn't something in the box or something I'd seen in the photos.

Rather, it was what was missing.

I carried the box into my room and pulled out the copies I had made of the accident report. Extracting the inventory sheet, I compared the list with the box. The only things that were missing didn't matter. The bloodied clothes he had been wearing. The truck's instruction manual.

I flopped onto my bed, the police report to one side of me and Dean's belongings on the other. Something was right there in my mind, right on the edge of my vision. Something important.

I sat up and looked at the pile of photos that had spilled out onto the covers. *That awful graduation tassel twisting and turning in the wind...*

A tingle ran along my arm, goose bumps racing across my skin. That's what was missing. The thing he valued. The thing he wouldn't have been without. He had scrimped and saved for it.

Dean had played baseball that spring, just like every year since he was a little kid. In a late-season game, a batter hammered a line drive. Reacting without thinking, Dean caught the ball with his bare hand rather than his glove. The impact broke two fingers, he proudly recounted that night at the dinner table, but he'd fielded the ball and stopped a base runner from advancing. Without that catch, they would have lost. Dean was, once again, the hero.

The trainer examined his injured hand. By the time they reached the hospital, he warned, the doctors would have to cut the class ring off his swollen fingers. Dean refused to let that happen. He gripped the ring, grimaced, and tugged.

When he came home from the doctor's office, his hand was splinted and bandaged. His dented class ring dangled from a chain given to him by a nurse.

He never left home without it. That chain hung around his neck unless he was playing sports or working in the fields. Then, it was hooked over the rearview mirror of his truck. The day before high school graduation, I had sat at my window watching Dean and Dad work on the tractor. Dean was shirtless and grease covered. The glint of the ring in the sunlight caught my eye as it twisted from the rearview mirror.

That night as he drove out of the VFW, it hung there, sparkling in the streetlights. He hadn't wanted to risk it falling off in the crowded party.

I scanned the police report again, but I knew I wouldn't find it. It hadn't been in his truck when the police arrived at the scene of the accident.

Had he left it at Blake's? Or maybe the impact of the crash had thrown it from the mirror. A rescuer, in the chaos, might have stepped on it and trampled it into the ground. I vowed to search the next day.

Trampled? Someone had left those footprints around the truck. *Would they have taken it?* That made little sense. *Unless…*

I jumped to my feet. A few days earlier, I had seen a ring. It had bothered me because it was somewhere unexpected. The person who had it never expected me to see it.

For the second night in a row, I left my house in the dark.

33

W ith no traffic on the road, driving downtown didn't take long. I parked at Sammy's Pub and wondered if Blake was inside. But I wasn't here to socialize. I hoped parking my garish SUV among the smattering of cars would hide it from anyone who might notice.

Eyeing the sidewalks devoid of any pedestrians at this time of night, I whispered a silent thanks that I still wore Dean's bulky denim coat. If someone saw me during the block-and-a-half walk to Stewart's Consignment, they would only remember a bigger guy in that coat. Without that camouflage, a skinny, tattooed rocker would be too memorable.

As I approached the store, I hoped Xander had never changed the locks. Because we spent so much time rehearsing in the building, Anna had given me a key to come and go as I pleased. I wasn't sure Xander knew. I wouldn't have hidden it from him back then, but I didn't think we'd ever talked about it either. He lived only a few blocks away, so when I was meeting him at the store, he always beat me and had the door open. I'd kept the key as a reminder of my happy times playing with the Wicked Centipedes. On lonely nights on the road, it was small source of comfort to see it on my key ring, so I had kept it.

The key slipped easily into the lock on the front door and turned without hesitation. The click echoed in the empty street. A glance around assured me no one was watching. Holding my breath, I pulled open the door and waited for the shriek of a burglar alarm. None rang out.

Score another point for small town safety.

I slipped inside the dark store and flipped the lock closed behind me. I stumbled through the cluttered aisles as far back as I could before the faint glow from the streetlight outside faded to black. Thinking I was far enough away from the window to avoid being spotted, I turned on the flashlight on my cell phone. Its beam guided me through the curtain and into the rear of the store. I moved around the file cabinets to Xander's desk and examined the contents on the wall. The photos. The high school diploma. But what I was looking for was no longer there.

On my first visit earlier in the week, a class ring had hung on a chain from the diploma. At the time, I'd thought nothing of it. Plenty of kids in our senior class had bought them. But I'd ridiculed it. And so had my best friend. Xander and I had sat alone at our lunch table, laughing at the absurdity of such a trinket. We were cooler than the cool kids. We didn't need anything to remind us of high school.

If I'd thought about it then, I probably would have guessed someone had come into the store to sell their old ring. Maybe Blake, having drunk away his last paycheck. And maybe it was whoever had taken Dean's ring.

But if that was true, why would Xander hide it? The second day, I'd sat back here with Xander but never noticed the ring was gone. He hadn't sold it, because it hadn't been out front in a display case. He'd had it on his memento wall. Then he'd removed it when I showed up.

Why display something he thought was ridiculous to own? Why would he hide it as soon as I returned?

The answer was painfully obvious now. The ring meant something to him that I wasn't supposed to see.

I hoped he hadn't thrown it away. Or taken it home to hide. I needed it to prove I hadn't imagined the whole thing. And that it really was Dean's and not just some random ring.

I only hoped it was still in the store, carefully hidden until I left town again. And I was sure if he had kept it all these years, it was important enough to him to keep now.

I turned my attention to the desk drawers. They were locked, but I had been prepared for that. From my many hours helping Anna, I knew a toolbox sat on the workbench in the corner for simple repairs for consigned items. A set of screwdrivers waited on the top. A flathead made quick work of the flimsy desk lock. I opened the thin top drawer and sorted through its contents. Pencils. Pens. Paper. The usual.

The side drawer held a stapler, tape dispenser, scissors, and rulers. That left the bottom file drawer. I had seen a coffee thermos, a bag lunch, and various snacks, so it was where he stored his food for the day. When I opened it, as I expected, those items were gone. He would take them home each night to clean and reuse the next day.

But with nothing else in the drawer, I had a clear view of the manila envelope lying on the bottom. I extracted it and shook the contents into my hand. A cheap chain with a Millerton High School class ring with a dent like a baseball would make if caught barehanded.

With trembling hands, I held the ring between my fingers and shined the flashlight. Engraved along the interior were three letters. *DTM 2006.*

Dean Thomas McDougal. Class of 2006.

Squeezing my hand around it, I collapsed into the chair

and let the tears flow. Why would my best friend steal my brother's most valuable keepsake?

Xander had gotten his hands on it between the time Dean left the VFW parking lot and the time the police inventoried the contents of the truck. The only logical answer was that he'd taken it from the accident site. The boot prints around Dean's truck belonged to him.

But the logical answer wasn't logical at all. Why would he stand there and watch my brother die? Why not help?

That left the worst question of all. What was Xander doing driving that road early on a Sunday morning, so far from his home?

He hadn't happened upon the accident. Somehow, some-way, he'd caused it. *But why?*

The sheriff's department was a block away. I should deliver the ring to them right now. I didn't know how to explain how I'd found it inside this store, though. I wasn't a lawyer, but I was fairly sure having a years-old key wasn't a defense against a breaking-and-entering charge. Even if I didn't get charged, the ring might not be usable as evidence. I'd watched many an episode of *Law and Order* on lonely nights, and something told me a judge would toss it from court.

I couldn't put it back and let them come get it the next day, though. Xander would know someone had broken into his desk. I couldn't fix that. He would guess it was me. He would get rid of the ring.

Besides, I didn't want someone else to confront Xander. With my newfound backbone, I wanted to look him in the eye and demand answers. But not tonight. Not where he lived. If I even knew where that was.

One more night wouldn't matter. A seventeen-year-old secret could wait another day. So I slipped the ring and its chain into my pants pocket. I closed the desk drawer the best I could, but I didn't really try to hide that it had been opened.

With some perverse pleasure, I even imagined him sweating when he found the drawer had been jimmied.

I returned the screwdriver, slipped out the front door, and relocked it before walking back down the empty street to my waiting car.

34

The house was still dark when my mother shouted my name, her voice laced with panic. I'd been dreaming of confronting Xander with the ring and demanding an explanation, though I couldn't recall any excuse he offered that made any sense. Or any excuse at all. Maybe I'd just blocked it out. Or maybe my mind hadn't been able to come up with anything that made even dream logic.

When Mom called a second time, the dream vanished, and I sat up in bed. It was pitch-black outside the window. I couldn't figure out if I was awake or still dreaming. Disoriented, I fumbled for my cell phone resting on the bedside table and checked the time: 4:18 a.m.

I sat up, rubbed sleep from my eyes, and turned on the lamp. Dean's denim coat hung across the back of the chair. The chain and Dean's ring lay on the desk where I had left them the night before. I had twisted it in my hands, slipped it on and off my finger, and studied those initials for hours before finally collapsing in exhaustion. I couldn't help but reach out and touch it again. The cold metal sent a shiver up my spine.

Mom called again from the base of the steps, pushing me fully awake.

"Coming," I shouted as I slipped on the jeans I had worn the night before. After pulling the sweatshirt over my head, I stumbled barefooted out of my room.

When I reached the top of the stairs, I froze at the sight of my mother's tear-stained face staring up from the first floor. She wore a robe over her nightclothes and leaned against the wall.

I raced down the steps just in time to catch her in my arms as she sagged toward the floor. I feared I already knew the answer, but I begged her to tell me what was going on. She blubbered, the words confused and slurred.

I raised her to her feet and guided her to the couch, pushing the blanket she slept under to the corner of the cushions. Once I had her settled so she wouldn't collapse to the floor, I asked her again, "What's wrong?"

She opened her mouth to speak, but nothing came out. She looked lost and alone, and I felt such pain for her. I gathered her into a hug and let her cry against my shoulder.

When her sobs subsided, I gently sat her back against the couch. She tried again to speak but couldn't. Instead, with a shaking hand, she pointed toward the rear parlor.

I squeezed her hand and urged her to wait on the couch for me to return. With more dread than I had ever felt, I forced my feet forward and entered the darkened room. I reached for the light switch then decided against flipping it. The light coming from the lamp in the next room was enough to let me know what had happened. Dad was pale and still. His eyes were closed, but his chest no longer rose and fell. After his long battle, he had slipped away quietly in his sleep.

I felt a tear roll down my cheek. *We never got to say goodbye. How fitting.*

MY FATHER WAS AS ORGANIZED in death as he had been in life. A folder in a desk drawer contained everything we needed, including step-by-step instructions from hospice.

The first phone call set the machinery of death into motion. Fire department medics arrived with flashing red lights and confirmed the obvious. Dad had been a volunteer with the department for years. Both of the first responders knew him and his wishes. The do-not-resuscitate order in his file was perfunctory.

They radioed to cancel the ambulance and shut off their strobes as a sheriff's deputy pulled into the drive. He asked a few questions and offered his condolences. By the time the medical examiner cleared the scene, the funeral home workers had arrived. The body was respectfully carried out of the house and driven away.

The driveway was again empty. The house fell silent. My tough, strong mother, who had always been the foundation of our family, wilted. I helped her dress. Made her eat some breakfast despite her protests that she couldn't possibly. Bundled her into my rental car and carefully snapped the seat belt into place around her.

I drove her to the funeral home and sat with her as she nodded numbly in answer to questions, mostly confirming what she and Dad had already decided. He had even made all the payments. The obituary was prewritten and we only needed to add the date of death, but even that made her cry all over again.

She was, for the first time in over four decades, alone in the world without her partner. My heart ached for her through each step of the process.

The preacher, Reverend Jacob Brawley, a different one from when Dean had died, arrived and prayed with her. He assured her that everything would be handled as they had discussed. He introduced himself to me, his big hands engulfing mine in a firm handshake.

When we were finally done, I got her to stumble back to my car and drove her home. Russ's pickup truck waited in the driveway. He and Sarah rose from their seats on the porch and came down the steps. She hugged my mother and helped her up the steps and inside, urging her the entire way to eat some lunch to keep up her strength.

Once they were inside, Russ said, "Sorry about your dad."

He shook my hand, and I mumbled my thanks. We settled into the rocking chairs on the porch. The frenetic energy of the morning seeped out of my body, replaced by a deep tiredness. Not just the early start of the day or the lateness of the night before had zapped me. The awfulness of everything consumed me. A man I'd barely thought of a week earlier had died and left a gaping hole in me. Would I have felt this much pain if I hadn't come home? Despite the agony, though, I was glad I had.

As I relaxed, my mind could think of the things I'd left undone.

Just the day before, I had promised both Sarah and Russ that I wouldn't hurt Harrison. He would expect me to join him for our day's jam session. I should have called and told him what had happened.

"Don't worry. As soon as we heard the news, we figured you wouldn't be there. Harrison totally understands," Russ assured me. "He's at the house watching his brother and sister so Sarah and I can be here."

We rocked in silence for several moments before Russ said, "I'm sorry Skeeter never got to hear it, but Harrison is okay with telling your mom. When you think she's ready, of course."

I nodded. Not yet. Not today. But before the funeral. I wasn't running from it.

But one thing must get handled today. I wrapped my fingers around the ring in my pocket.

In small towns, news traveled fast, so maybe Xander already knew of Dad's death. Maybe he was so disconnected from people he hadn't heard. Either way, he would have seen the jimmied desk drawer as soon as he got to the store. Would have known the envelope was empty when he opened the drawer. Would know what had been found. Would have suspected it was me who had taken it.

I explained to Russ that I had an errand I needed to handle without giving him a reason.

He didn't pry. Without even knowing what I was doing, he asked, "Want me to go with you?"

The thought of having Russ back me up gave me strength, just like Dean had always done, even if I'd been too blind to notice. But this one, I needed to handle on my own, so I declined.

"Whatever you need, Little Mac."

The nickname no longer bothered me at all.

35

W hen I arrived at Stewart's Consignments, everything looked normal from the outside. The lights glowed. The front doors stood open. Xander sat on the stool at the cash register, the newspaper on the counter in front of him. But as the electronic chime announced my entrance, he didn't stir and never looked up. The newspaper was still folded closed.

I marched across the room and placed the ring on the counter. He stared at it for a moment before reaching out and touching it with his finger. He raised his head so that I could see his eyes were red and swollen from crying.

"I should've guessed my mom gave you a key." His voice cracked.

"She trusted me. Like I did you."

His eyes dropped back to the counter. His finger traced the outline of the ring, caressing it. His voice was barely audible, even in the silence of the store. "We used to make fun of people buying class rings. How meaningless they were. How high school sucked. Who would want to remember? Unless, of course, those years were as good as it was going to get."

I remembered. I had wallowed in my outcast status. "What changed?"

He wiped his sleeve across his face. "The most horrid realization hit me. Those were my best years. Playing drums in this store. Watching you play your guitar. Listening to Sarah sing. But you were both leaving, and I was stuck here. Things were never going to be better for me."

I snorted in frustration. "You could have gone to college."

"Please. My grades sucked. I didn't play sports. Didn't have money. They don't take people like me."

"You had to have some money. Your mom had this store."

Xander waved his arms around him. "What did we have? The inventory is consignment. The building is a rental. We barely sold enough to keep the doors open and the lights on. If we had any left over at the end of the month, it went to the mortgage on the house or food. Mom even had taken a second mortgage I didn't know about. We were always behind on bills."

"You think I had money?"

"Some you'd squirreled away from playing down in Asheville." He looked up at me. "But mostly, you had talent. Mediocre drummers like me are a dime a dozen. There was no future for me in music."

I slammed my hand down on the counter, making the ring jump. "Do you think it's been easy for me? I struggle to earn enough money to survive. Played until my fingers bled. And I have squat to show for it."

"But you left. You still got a chance. You gonna honestly tell me that your life hasn't been better since high school?"

I couldn't say that. Although things hadn't worked out the way I'd planned, I'd still had some pretty cool days. Playing music. Hearing crowds. Seeing the country.

When I didn't answer, he looked back down at the ring and continued. "And I thought Sarah was leaving too."

"But she didn't. She stayed here."

"Because…" He looked down at his hands. "I always thought it was Dean's."

"He. Not it. His name is Harrison. And he's a good kid."

"And he's yours." Contempt dripped off his tongue as he said it. A tear dripped off his cheek. "I never even suspected."

I clenched my fists and groaned. "But you didn't even know she was pregnant that day. No one knew. Not even her. So that doesn't explain why you have this ring, does it?"

He shook his head and whispered, "No."

"So, what? You took the ring because you wanted to remember high school?"

"No." He swallowed hard. He tried to look at me, but he couldn't. His eyes kept falling to the counter. "I didn't even know I took it."

"You're not making sense." I leaned against the counter so he couldn't avoid my glare. "What were you even doing out there? Where Dean wrecked?"

He whispered, "I followed him."

I had expected his admission, known it was coming, but the words still shocked me. "But why? What did Dean have to do with anything?"

He choked back a sob. "Everything. He was the freaking king of everything."

"You hated him enough to kill him?"

"I didn't…" He swallowed and hesitated, searching for the right words. "It was an accident. I didn't mean for it to happen."

I hadn't wanted to hit someone in a long time. Not since that night with Dean. In that moment, though, I could see my fist slamming into Xander's face. Instead, I clenched my teeth. "But you did cause it."

"I didn't mean to."

I clenched my jaw. "Talk."

After a long moment of silence, he finally spoke. His voice was low and monotone. "Mom was sleeping late because it was a Sunday. It was the only day of the week she didn't open the store, so she could sleep as late as she wanted."

"I was still jazzed from the concert the night before. It had been epic. Like, probably the best night of my life. But I was also fired up because I'd seen the fight between you and Dean. And I knew it was about Sarah. I'd seen him talking to her."

I could picture him bounding down the steps. Making coffee. Maybe whistling because he was so happy about the concert. While waiting for the coffee to brew, he would have crossed the room to the window with the blinds, peeled them open, and peeked over at Sarah's house.

"She sat rocking in the chair, a book cradled in her hand. She was beautiful. The most beautiful girl I'd ever seen. And she spoke to me, you know? But my time was running out. She wasn't from Millerton. She had only spent the year here because her mother died. In just a couple of months, she was leaving. Headed off for college. She'd meet some handsome frat guy, fall in love, get married, raise a family. Probably, he'd be a doctor or lawyer or schoolteacher, or even maybe a singer. And she'd forget all about me."

He stared blankly out the front plate-glass window of the store. "But that night before—up on that stage. The loud music. The lights. We were gods for a night, you know? And maybe, I thought, I needed to stop being a coward. Tell her how I felt. Take a chance, or I'd be stuck in this god-awful town all alone."

As he made himself a bowl of cereal that morning, he vowed to make the best of the summer. To have as much fun as he could before I left to make music and Sarah left for college. With his breakfast eaten, he poured a second cup of coffee and planned to return to his room. On his way, he paused to gaze once again at Sarah on her porch.

But she was no longer alone. Dean was leaning against the porch support, chatting with her.

"He was grinning like he always did. King of the world. And then..." He choked. "She stood up. He pushed off that post. They hugged."

I knew now what Xander never did. That hug wasn't about her and Dean. It was about her and me. Dean had apologized for the night before because he didn't know we were dating. He'd congratulated her. And hugged her.

Then he'd turned, bounded down the steps to his truck. With a goodbye wave and that smile beaming, he started his truck and drove off. She smiled back, waved at him, then disappeared into the house.

"My heart broke. I thought they had made a date. The chance I had that summer with her was gone. Because of him."

"So you went after him?"

"I didn't..." He looked down. "I grabbed my mother's car keys from her purse. She would sleep for another couple of hours. I'd be back before she woke up. I didn't have a plan. I was just going to talk to him. To tell him I saw her first. Had always been there for her."

It was like he was a little kid calling dibs. "You didn't own her."

"I know. The more we drove, the more I realized how stupid I was being. But I couldn't stop myself. I knew he was going home. I knew that road as well as both of you did. I knew once you got past those curves, those roads straightened up. My mom's Camaro was old, but it could take his Silverado in that stretch. I could get in front of him. Block his path. Make him stop. Tell him how I felt."

I could picture it in my mind. The sports car hugging the curves far enough behind Dean that he would never have noticed it. Dean fiddling with the radio dial. Looking up only when he heard the roar of the overtaking car.

"What happened?"

Xander shook his head. The tears were still flowing, his mouth opening and closing.

I asked again. "What went wrong?"

He stammered. "I cut too close. Hit the brakes. I…"

Dean wouldn't have expected that. He would have assumed the passing car would keep going, disappearing out of sight around the next bend. In his hesitation, the truck would have closed the gap between it and the car in front of it. He would have slammed on the brakes hard to avoid hitting it. The weight of the truck. The wet road.

"I could see him in my mirror. Fighting the steering wheel for control. The pickup fishtailed. The right wheels dropped off the pavement. The truck yanked right and disappeared from view. It careened into the trees. I heard this thunderous crash of metal and glass. By the time I got stopped and looked back, all I saw was the crumpled truck wrapped in a haze of smoke."

I shuddered in horror at the image. That tassel swinging from the rearview mirror. Blood dripping on the seat.

After several minutes of silence, Xander spoke softly. "I turned around. Pulled beside the wreckage and jumped out. Ripped open his door. Tried to get him out. Tried to save him. I swear to God I wanted to help, but he was so mangled."

"Was he breathing?"

"Yes. But he couldn't talk. I don't think he knew anything, if that makes any difference."

It didn't.

Xander lowered his head. "I ran around to the other side. I don't know why. It made no sense when I thought about it later, but I was panicking. Leaned in. Tried to figure out what to do. And then…"

"Then?"

"He just stopped. No noise. Just the ticking of the engine. Some cows mooing out in the distance. And that awful smell of hot radiator fluid on the ground." He squeezed his eyes shut. "I've had nightmares about it ever since."

Good. I hoped he had nightmares for the rest of his miserable life. "Why didn't you call for help?"

"I didn't have a cell phone back then. Not even sure if you could get reception out there."

"You could have gone to the barn. They were in there milking cows. They would have had a phone or been able to get you to one."

"It wouldn't have made a difference."

"It might have. We'll never know." I took a deep breath and steadied myself for the rest. "Go on."

He couldn't meet my eyes. "I drove back toward town, looking for a pay phone. The first one I saw was in the parking lot of Abe's Market. I pulled up beside it and reached for the door handle. That's when I realized I had it." He shuddered and touched the ring on the counter. "The class ring was in my hand."

"Why did you take it?"

"I don't know. I don't even remember taking it. I was going to turn around and go put it back."

"Why didn't you?"

"The volunteer fire department alarm went off. I sat there, debating what to do, until a highway patrol car passed with its blue lights and siren blaring, a fire truck right behind it. No need to call. I knew where they were going. And I couldn't go back then."

"Yeah, you could have." I clenched my fist. "So, what did you do?"

"Went home. Took a shower. Bagged up my clothes and threw them in the dumpster behind my mom's store."

"You covered up the crime."

"No, I swear. I just… panicked. I was so scared."

I picked up the ring and held it in my hand. "If you weren't trying to hide it, why didn't you tell me? I deserved to know what happened."

"I couldn't bring myself to go out to your house. I figured I would wait until after the funeral. Or maybe I was just making excuses. Probably. But it didn't matter, because you left before I got the chance."

Tears streamed down his face, but I couldn't muster even the slightest sympathy for him. The flimsy excuse of blaming his secret on my leaving was familiar enough to me. It wasn't much different from the way I blamed everyone but myself for things that happened to me.

Keeping the secret bottled up may have tormented him, but that didn't outweigh the loss of my brother. I turned my back on him and headed toward the open front doors.

His voice cracked behind me. "Please don't tell anyone."

"My mother deserves to know the truth. So did my father, but too late for that."

"But the police…"

I spun on my heel and glared at him. "You can go to them yourself. Or wait for them to come. I don't care."

His sobs echoed in my ears as I left the store.

36

I stood beside my father's coffin in front of the packed church. My hand trembled as I stroked the polished wood.

"You ready?" Russ stood at the front corner, his hand resting on the rail.

"Don't worry. We've got this." Blake gripped my shoulder. "Beautiful eulogy. You did Skeeter proud."

I nodded my thanks to them as they and the other four pallbearers lifted their heavy load. They followed the preacher down the church's aisle. I fell in behind them and offered my arm to my mother for support. Harrison, looking uncomfortable in a suit and tie, took her other arm. She had helped him tie it before coming to the church, a skill she thought her grandson should know.

The congregation fell in behind us. We marched out of the church, down the front steps, and across the cemetery to the waiting bier.

The smell of freshly turned dirt came to me as we settled into the chairs beside the open grave. I couldn't help but smile through my tears. The scent reminded me of my father, all the times he'd come into the house after a long day in the field, tired but proud of his work.

The preacher spread his arms and intoned, "Let us pray."

I draped my arm over my mother's shoulder and bowed my head. My car was waiting for me, but it wasn't packed yet. Plenty of time to get ready for the next day's flight. Right now, though, my place was here. I wasn't slinking away again.

Besides, we had an impressive spread of food waiting back at the house for the mourners. I planned to eat my fill and listen to Dad's many friends tell their stories about him. I had already heard dozens over the last few days. Helping to round up someone's loose cattle. Joining a crew barn-raising after a fellow farmer suffered a fire. Delivering food to a church, feeding people who had been flooded out of their homes one rainy spring. Always a man of few words, but always there when people needed him.

I wished I had taken the time before to hear the stories. I would like to have known them while he was still alive. But the past couldn't be changed. Only the future.

And so I was thinking of the future. Those closest to me knew my plans. By the end of the day, everyone would.

Except Xander. I hadn't seen him since leaving his store and walking the block and a half to the sheriff's department. I sat down in the sheriff's office, laid Dean's class ring on his desk, and told him what I knew. I couldn't prove a word of it, but the story was out there.

The sheriff stopped by the house that evening. He let us know they'd gone down to the store and found Xander sitting at his drum set. Not playing, just sitting there. He'd given a full confession.

They'd turned everything over to the district attorney to decide his fate. He probably wouldn't face a long incarceration, if he even went to jail. He didn't have a record. The accident itself wasn't intentional, even if his pursuit of Dean was. And in all the intervening years, he hadn't been in any other trouble.

But in small towns, punishment came in other ways. The store hadn't reopened and probably never would. People had already rushed to reclaim their consigned goods.

The soft whir of the motors brought my thoughts back to the cemetery. The coffin lowered gently into the ground until it disappeared into the shadows. The congregation broke, some stopping by my mother and me to offer their condolences. Others drifted to their cars, knowing they would see us later at the house.

As the crowd thinned, I noticed Blake kneeling on the ground. He gently touched Dean's marker only a few feet away from my father's. Blake's finger outlined the epitaph as single tear slipped down his cheek.

A beloved friend who had protected his buddy simply by being there for him.

The beloved son would lie beside his dad. The two of them were probably already discussing the coming harvest. The thought made me smile.

I was late to the game, but Dean was a beloved brother. My brother. I was a McDougal, one of a long line of McDougals.

37

Tracking down my old friends in Asheville, the ones I used to busk with, wasn't easy. But once I found the first one, things began to fall into place. He knew a few of the others and shared their phone numbers. When I contacted them, they helped me find more.

After emptying out my old apartment, I came back to Asheville. I enjoyed the hustle of working on the street again. Watching the crowds smile. Hearing coins clink as they landed in the guitar case. The camaraderie of the performers, supporting and protecting each other.

But I couldn't play the streets every night. Most nights, I was working.

Turned out that Charlie had done far better than I'd ever imagined. He'd parlayed his street earnings into a food truck that funded a coffee shop that had expanded into a small art gallery and a licensed bar. Typical eclectic Asheville, where a tourist could wander in off the street, admire paintings and sculptures, sip a coffee, and eat a pastry or enjoy a locally brewed beer with a hot sandwich—all from the same entrepreneur.

Finding reliable help was always Charlie's biggest problem, but I'd long ago learned a strong work ethic by practicing so many hours on my guitar. And now that I had quit quitting, he could rely on me.

It could be busy some nights, bouncing between ringing up an art sale, slicing a piece of pie, or pouring a cold beer, but I loved interacting with the crowds. By the time I finally traipsed up the steps to the small apartment above the store, I would collapse from exhaustion.

One of the bonuses was that Millerton was only a half hour away, close enough to visit as often as I wanted—which was surprisingly often—though still far enough away to let me enjoy a little more urban life. Dad had been right. I wasn't cut out for the farming life. But that was okay.

My favorite part of my job was booking musical entertainment. Live music every evening drew people through the doors. Just like he had done for me, Charlie believed firmly in finding talented musicians starting in their careers or who hadn't yet had their lucky breaks and giving them a chance. The music business was hard—I knew that better than anyone. For most of them, playing would never be much more than a side gig, but at least they would get to play in front of an audience.

Tonight was a special one for me. I'd been planning it for a long time, working out details and making sure the performance would go well. My nerves were on high alert as show-time approached.

I'd had to wait until my mother was ready to venture out for the first time since Dad passed. She sat at the reserved front table, enjoying a sandwich I made special for her and a glass of iced tea sweetened to her liking. When I had invited her, she struggled to remember the last time she had been out to a restaurant, much less to Asheville. She had agonized over what to wear, though I kept assuring her it didn't matter.

Beside her, Blake sipped a cup of coffee. He was trying, again, to break old habits. If he succeeded, we would cheer him. If he failed, we would be there for him. That was what friends did.

Rounding out the foursome were Russ and Sarah, fidgeting as they picked at the deserts I'd placed in front of them. Russ looked as uncomfortable as my father would have been sitting in some coffeehouse in Asheville. But he was there. I respected that.

When they finished their meals and were settled, it was time for the music to begin. A healthy crowd had gathered in the restaurant. When I stepped out onto the small stage and approached the microphone, the conversations dropped to a low murmur.

My spiel most nights was a brief welcome to the crowd and introduction of the performer, but tonight's was a little longer. I explained how special the evening was for me. Pointing to the front table, I welcomed my guests and thanked them for coming, ignoring my mother's blush and dab of her eyes as I acknowledged my brother and father and how their impact had led to me being on that stage.

Then I stepped back as the house lights dropped, and a spot illuminated the performer. He wiped the perspiration off his face then positioned his fingers on the guitar strings. With the first chords rising above the crowd, I could see his nerves settle. His voice joined, soft and melodic. The familiar ballad had everyone in the crowd swaying. A fast song had the crowd's toes tapping. A slow, melancholy one brought on a few tears.

Then came the moment. Playing covers of familiar songs went well in bars and restaurants. Original songs, though, were always riskier. The audience wouldn't know what to expect. The unfamiliar could throw them.

But the song worked as beautifully as I anticipated. The

vocals were strong. The rhythm was fast and challenging but perfectly executed. When the last note faded, the crowd cheered. They wanted an encore.

From the shadows, I couldn't help but swell with pride as Harrison gave them one more song.

D.K. WALL NEWSLETTER

If you enjoyed this book, please subscribe to my FREE monthly newsletter.

The newsletter contains fun stories, an amusing reader survey, weird facts, and, yes, news about upcoming books. If you decide it's not for you, simply unsubscribe. No questions. No fuss.

Just for trying, you'll receive a free gift (or two). For details, visit:

dkwall.com/subscribe

ACKNOWLEDGMENTS

Trapped in my house in the early days of the pandemic, I found an escape from the stress and uncertainty in my usual places—books and music. Craving normalcy, I watched entirely too many hours of rock concerts, from classics to modern day. Thank you, YouTube, for keeping me distracted.

One quiet night, *The Vamps* danced and sang on my computer screen. The four friends had spent their teenaged years performing on stages around the world. Many of those shows had been recorded and posted online. Their energy was electrifying. The positive spirit was just what I needed to get through those quiet nights wondering when the world might return to normal.

With arenas and stadiums closed, their entire lives were on hold, just like the rest of us. They were sitting at home rather than traveling the globe and playing their music. When things came back to life, would their careers resume? Or would their fans have moved on?

As I pondered those questions, Freddie McDougal was born. He wasn't a star. Most of the musicians I've known toiled away in relative obscurity, playing bars and weddings scheduled around their day jobs.

A few, though, were just a break away from hitting stardom. One different decision and they would have been stars.

I pulled out a notebook and began scratching out notes. Piece by piece, Freddie came to life. I learned about his family, his brother, his chances, and his mistakes.

Now don't worry about *The Vamps*. They released their fifth album in the fall of 2020 and returned to the stage in 2021, but not everyone fared as well.

An acquaintance landed a huge role in a revival of a play on Broadway just before the pandemic, an opportunity that would have catapulted her career. When the theaters closed, she hoped that things would resume in a few weeks or months, just like we all did. But as time dragged on, returning the show to the stage became impossible. The production was canceled and her role evaporated.

Of course, the same thing happened to untold numbers of people outside the arts. College students lost internships and starting jobs. Companies failed and careers were derailed.

I didn't want to write about a pandemic. (Or I should say, not again. A very few of you may have read the serial story I wrote about a pandemic long before this came along. Maybe, I'll revisit that, but not yet.)

I did, however, want to write about Freddie. He intrigued me. I hope you enjoyed meeting him.

A huge thank you to everyone who helped me bring *Sour Notes* to life. Please indulge me for a moment while I name a few.

As always, a debt of gratitude goes to the amazing editing team at Red Adept—Lynn McNamee, Angie Lovell, Stefanie Spangler Buswell, and Libybet Rueda Gynn. As I wrestled the story out of my imagination, their questions and challenges made the finished product so much better. I can't imagine trying to do what I do without them.

Glendon Haddix of Streetlight Graphics listened to my description of the story and said he had an idea for a cover. Wow, did he ever. He captured both the loneliness and the serenity if the story.

My biggest thanks, as always, goes to my first reader, Todd Fulbright. Long before the first words are written, he listens to my ideas and asks the perfect questions. Don't worry, he's already asking questions about the next story coming down the pipe.

Finally, Dear Reader, thank you—for reading my books, for commenting on social media, for writing letters and emails, and for being so supportive.

Happy reading!

D.K. Wall

ABOUT THE AUTHOR

D.K. has lived his entire life in the Carolinas and Tennessee—from the highest elevations of the Great Smoky Mountains near Maggie Valley to the industrial towns of Gastonia and Hickory, the cities of Charlotte and Nashville, and the coastal salt marsh of Murrells Inlet.

Over the years, he's watched the textile and furniture industries wither and the banking and service industries explode, changing the face of the region. He uses his love of storytelling to share tales about the people and places affected.

Married and living in Asheville, surrounded by his family of rescued Siberian Huskies known as *The Thundering Herd*, D.K. takes the characters and tales of his lifetime of experience and remembers them better for your entertainment.

For more information and to enjoy his short stories and photographs, please visit the author's website:

dkwall.com

ALSO BY D. K. WALL

The Lottery

Jaxon With An X

Liars' Table

Sour Notes